KNIGHT DISCOVERER

Jayme Alencar de Oliveira Filho
& Jayme Sampaio Alencar

UNDERLINE
PUBLISHING

Knight
Discoverer
from darkness
to light

Contents

Knight
Discoverer
from darkness
to light

Prologue

4.5 billion years ago, planet Earth began taking form. Suddenly, a sizeable planet-like asteroid named Theia, nearly the size of Mars, hurtled towards Earth. Researchers assert that the Moon was formed when Theia, a proto-lunar impactor, collided with Earth, causing a ripple explosion and, creating a magnificent spark of light and dust surrounding the area. As the dust settled, a giant asteroid glided into the darkness of space. The remains drifted off and wouldn't be seen again for another 4.5 billion years.

By 2135, the indiscriminate use of natural resources and atmospheric pollution had left the world in disarray. Unscrupulous twenty-first-century politicians disregarded the scientific community's warnings. Now, the world was succumbing to its greed. This was what Earth looked like at the beginning of the twenty-first century.

Soon after the turn of the century, the world began to crumble. A calm and nurturing climate rapidly transformed into a wild environment and torrential storms, dust bowls, inundation, drought, and rising oceans. These calamities led to a dramatic decrease in the population, leaving the world a ghostly shell of its former self. All hope seemed lost, and the world desperately needed a savior. The populations panicked as states crumbled, and people felt their lives disintegrate.

But who would step foward and raise a helping hand? What would it take to reverse the damage done to the ecosphere? The desperate cries of the world were unmistakable. Yet, changing Earth's inhabitants' destinies and corrosive behaviors seemed unthinkable.

There's always an answer for everything happening under the sun - and all humanity's hope rests on the shoulders of a young man and his crew as they try to find a new home.

Alexander, an exceptionally talented young man and natural leader, was an excellent recruit for the International Space Command Center (ISCC). There, he met his love in a unique environment. Like his Catholic great-grandparents, he used science and faith to become a wise leader. His family motto was "God's Blessings and Hard Work." Alexander always lived by it. He even had it engraved on a bracelet given to him by his mother, Daisy.

As Alexander looked at a sandstorm forming over the horizon, where once a flourishing forest covered the landscape, he remembered his great-grandfather and the gift that could change people's future.

1
Joseph

Joseph was born in Brazil, the son of the proud Silva family, and immigrated to America. He was proud of both heritages, always working hard and taking every opportunity for success.

Joseph had become an astrophysicist and studied all the old and current concepts of astronomy and physics. However, he'd always been fascinated by—the Big Bang—the beginning of everything involved in life and everything around us—matter.

Joseph loved the mystery of the universe. When he was eight, he received a gift from his father, changing his life and future—an hourglass with the inscription, "Time is Relative. Brilliance is Not. From Darkness to Light." His father told him, "Joseph, I want you to have this. I hope it reminds you that no matter how dark sometimes may seem, we can always return to the light."

From that moment on, Joseph always kept the message of the inscription on the hourglass in his heart and mind. Something he would pass on to all of the Silvas yet to come, starting with his daughter, Daisy.

The beginning of the twenty-first century was a period of many uncertainties. Scientists discussed people felt their the rapid increase of pollution in the atmosphere with the accumulation of carbon dioxide (CO2). The building-up of greenhouse gases began raising the temperature to the point of no return for the Earth. Scientists were giving their warnings, but politicians wouldn't listen. This was when Joseph received this gift from his dad. Although concerned about the world's future, he was also optimistic about the ingenuity of the human spirit.

As Joseph grew up realized he wanted to achieve his childhood dream: becoming an astrophysecist. But he always remembered his dad's gift and the meaningful inscription. By the time Joseph finished his education, the worldwide weather had become more unpredictable, with more prolonged droughts and stronger storms. One day, he overheard an older couple in a discussion, and it piqued his interest. As he passed by an old shop in area, Joseph noticed they were engaged in a friendly conversation.

"It never used to be this long without the rain," the woman said before the gentleman replied, clad in an old, grey suit, "Yes, causing so many droughts worldwide. In the past two years, they have increased. This is insane!"

Joseph's curiosity made him stop and eavesdrop on the elderly couple. So, his thoughts had been correct; the droughts were more frequent, and something happened that caused all these shifts in the climate. Global warming destroyed the atmosphere, and humans could no longer stay silent; drastic action needed to occur, and Joseph was excited to find a solution.

He was a brilliant young man, recognized by his peers and colleagues as a man of expertise and wit. He was an immense fan of Albert Einstein, who revolutionized science at the start of the twentieth century with his relativity theory and many thought experiments (experiments carried out only in the imagination). Einstein was the first to create the idea of the universe not being just a space. Still, everything correlated and interconnected through a medium called the "space-time fabric" (fabric in which objects of the universe embed themselves), a new concept Einstein used to explain gravity's interaction of mass distorting the surrounding fabric.

The Big Bang theory states that the universe started from the point of massive and unimaginable pressure and gravity, where all the matter in the universe was concentrated into a point known as Singularity. We know that Singularity is the hypothesis that the invention of artificial super-intelligence will abruptly trigger massive technological growth, resulting in unfathomable changes to human civilization. But how could everything come from nothing?

Joseph was trying to elaborate on a new theory about space and time. He studied the old and current concepts of astronomy and physics but became fascinated by the start of everything—the Big Bang. He loved thought experiments and Einstein's idea of the Space-Time Fabric. This means that gravity is the interaction of mass distorting the fabric around them, which in turn creates orbits.

The distortion creates orbits just like the gravity wells (which result from the pull of gravity caused by a body in space, such as a planet). Using a coin for this concept is like throwing it inside a well. Following the curvature of the well, the coin travels until it falls to the bottom. The coin following the well's wall illustrates the distortion of objects with a significant mass cause in the space-time fabric. The distortion promotes the movement of planets around the sun. These gravitational waves were first detected and identified, proving Einstein's theory in 2016.

These changes speak of many creations to come from this intelligence. For example, the Big Bang could have created the universe, including its many features and life, a tech-driven Big Bang - with humans at the center of it all, resulting in creations that benefited humans.

Joseph continued to search for solutions in his head to solve complex problems.

In addition to being an astrophysicist, he was the father of a young girl named Daisy. One day, he took her to a park, and she went to jump on a trampoline. It seemed like a simple joke. But for him, always attentive to mental experiments, it would be the beginning of a new theory that would revolutionize the scientific world and the future of astrophysics.

He saw his lovely daughter jumping up and down on the trampoline, going higher and higher, and noted that the trampoline fabric was distorted as she landed on it.

He imagined his daughter would keep distorting the fabric until she would move to another place... another dimension... another universe.

What if his daughter kept jumping on the trampoline until she stretched it to a point where it could no longer be stretched? An ordinary mind would say she would fall to the ground. However, he didn't have a typical mind...

What would happen? Would she fall to the ground? His mind became wild with many imaginative ways to prevent the distortion and apply it to his thought experiment. Therefore, he imagined his daughter would keep distorting the fabric until, at one point, she would move to another place, another dimension, another universe. He started thinking. What distortions would affect the universe enough to design a fabric stretch throughout space? What was so massive that it could distort the fabric of space-time to the point of rupture?

The solution came to him like a bag of rocks slamming against his head – a black hole (a region of space-time where gravity is so strong that nothing – no particles or even electromagnetic radiation such as light – can escape from it); from this point of extreme gravity in the universe where light can't escape, there's an immense pull. Here, the black hole would squeeze all the matter into a singularity (a location where the quantities used to measure the gravitational field become infinite in a way that does not depend on the coordinate system). The Big Bang started with a singularity, and black holes ended in a singularity. Could there be a connection between both? At this moment, he remembered the gift his father gave him when he was eight years old. The hourglass is inscribed with the saying, "From Darkness to Light." Joseph wonders whether the "nothing" came from "something?" Like an hourglass, the matter could flow from one space to another. Perhaps a vast black hole would distort and disrupt the fabric of space-time to the point of rupture? Then, it would transfer all the matter absorbed by a black hole to another universe through a big bang event, "From Darkness to Light," "From Black Hole to Singularity."

In a single instant, his mind was open to the vastness of the universe. He was floating in the middle of the Milky Way Galaxy, looking straight into a monstrous black hole, a star called Sagittarius. Inside the singularity's black hole, through a tunnel funneled to another singularity, a wormhole to a brand-new Big Bang universe. He could see his thought experiment in his mind. The cosmos became a multiverse with many galaxies interacting with each other through destruction and creation. When he awoke from his reverie, feeling like an eternity had passed, Daisy was still jumping on the trampoline, unaware of the ground-breaking theory he had envisioned. She had become part of the beginning, part of history, playing a valuable role in guaranteeing she would prove his father's theory. Yet, she continued to jump, uncaring and enjoying her day.

"Dad?" When she spoke his name, the visions of galaxies dissipated, and all he saw was a tired daughter.

"Hey, Dad, can we go home? I'm done." She smiled, and his heart melted.

"Let's go; you've had enough for today. I am tired as well." She gave a short, contagious laugh and smiled, "I like it when you admit you get tired!" He looked to see a smile flicker across her face, showing gaps from the inevitable loss of teeth to the Tooth Fairy.

"So, you like it when I am tired?" he said.

"No, I didn't think you ever became tired. You are always moving and thinking."

"That may be true, but I'm older and don't need as much sleep. Sweatheart, when you exercise you become tired. It's good for your body but remember you must sleep well to rest both the body and the mind – especially when you're little."

"Whatever!" She smiled back at him. Joseph smiled at her, too, but his mind became caught up in a world of black holes. Understanding the process,

Joseph knew he had an enormous task in front of him. The ground-breaking work ahead of him would take a lifetime, but success was the only option.

Joseph's battle was to complete the puzzle in his mind. But in science, sometimes the puzzle gets completed long after the trials, bringing the equation straight to writing; it would take time. He was conceiving, researching, hypothesizing, theorizing, and putting all the calculations into a comprehensive theory.

"Sorry, Daisy... just off in thought. I'm getting tired. I think you jumped enough for today.

"What were you thinking about?"

"Oh...something that would change the perspective of everything. Something that's going to be very hard to prove."

"Don't worry, Dad. You're the smartest guy I know. If anyone can do it, you can."

"With that amount of confidence, I'll be able to do anything."

"Like, make us your famous Feijoada in time for dinner tonight?"

"Now you're pushing it... but I'll certainly try." "Yes!" They both laughed as they walked off down the path.

As Daisy and Joseph journeyed back home, the time seemed short.

Joseph knew the journey he was about to undertake would separate him from his daughter.

However, he was also aware of the personal difficulties and sacrifices he would have to make.

In the end, Joseph believed saving the world was necessary. He hoped that she would come to accept and appreciate his mission and sacrifice in the future, knowing that he did all of this for her and the greater good of humanity.

Knight
Discoverer
from darkness
to light

2
Singularity

Joseph started working on his theory. He had big questions to answer - what if the universe is inside a black hole, and the dark energy continues to expand? Would the universe's matter absorb into the black hole into another universe? Would singularity be the same type as in the Big Bang, and can they connect it to a wormhole?

The wormhole solved the Einstein field equations for gravity. It acts the same as "tunnels" by connecting the points in space and time. Thus, wormholes could allow space travelers to travel between two points (say, Earth and Mars) and complete the journey as quickly as traveling to outer space.

This concept of an expanding universe was proved and established by the famous twentieth-century astronomer Edwin Hubble in 1929, where he found that the universe was not static but expanding. More recent analyses have shown this rate of expansion speeding up.

Expanding the universe is like someone blowing a balloon. The balloon would get larger and larger until no more air or matter was available. Thus, the rate of expansion would be the rate of the balloon being blown.

So, Joseph continued working hard to develop his mathematical formulas to begin his procedures:

· Expansion Rate = Velocity Rate of Matter being sucked by the black hole. (ER = BHMv).

· Black hole matter = visible matter + dark matter + dark energy. (BHM=VM+DM+DE).

· Black Hole & Big Bang (B.H. & B.B.)

By calculating the exact size of a black hole, he could create an alternative universe with a new equation, {Black hole size = Space/ Time (13.7billion years) + visible matter + dark matter + dark energy} [BHs=S/T+VM+DM+DE]. Earth's increased heat, drought, and insect outbreaks are all linked to climate change; it is just the start of the calamity wreaking havoc on the world. Essential daily needs will evaporate; declining water supplies, reduced agricultural yields, and health effects in cities due to heat, flooding, and erosion in coastal areas will put Earth on the brink of extinction. But if this formula could come to fruition, it may save Earth's people.

Overjoyed by the hope that this formula could work, Joseph continued to exact all the needed information. He knew the method would work whether the data got lost inside a black hole. Knowing the work of Antoine Lavoisier, who named and determined oxygen was the fundamental substance in combustion. He also established the law of conservation of mass and decided that combustion and respiration caused by chemical reactions with oxygen proved that black holes transferred data to other universes but did not absorb them. Therefore, Joseph also believed that nothing leaves in nature by transforming everything from chemical elements to entire galaxies.

He thought, "Is this crazy? Is it that logical and straightforward? How am I going to prove this outlandish idea? Does multiverse (an imaginary collection of diverse visible universes, each of which would include everything available by a linked community of spectators) theory explain what I'm trying to create?"

Indeed, proving these things will be tricky, especially when figuring out how to translate one's mind to paper. The process must be seamless, and people must understand the underlying crisis, respond well to the research, and execute the transition. Proven science allows the world to know everything presented to them will work - this theory will inspire the world. Joseph hoped he would get the chance to face the world.

Initially, the process began on a rocky path; his progression was complex. He became the joke of the science community, ridiculed and ostracized by the same colleagues and institutions that one day would applaud him for his achievements in astrophysics.

One day, in the dimly lit lecture hall of the university, palpable anticipation hung in the air as Joseph took his place at the front. Before him sat a congregation of curious minds, ready to grapple with the enigma he was about to unveil. The atmosphere crackled with intellectual energy as Joseph prepared to challenge the very foundations of their understanding.

"So, the grand question I'm grappling with is... what if our universe exists within the confines of a black hole, and the mysterious dark energy propelling our cosmic expansion is matter continuously drawn from another universe?" Joseph's voice resonated, breaking the silence.

His colleagues, a sea of raised eyebrows and exchanged glances, seemed skeptical yet intrigued.

"If my hypothesis holds water, the singularity of a black hole mirrors the singularity of our Big Bang. The connection? A cosmic wormhole," he continued undeterred.

The room buzzed with murmurs as a colleague voiced a familiar inquiry, "Hubble's expanding universe theory, right?"

With a confident smile, Joseph responded, "No longer a mere theory. The universe isn't static; it's expanding and accelerating as we speak."

Turning to the chalkboard, he swiftly inscribed complex equations. When he faced the audience again, the passage of time had etched itself upon him, adding years to his countenance.

"Expansion rate equals the velocity of matter being drawn into the black hole," he whispered. "Black hole matter comprises visible matter, dark matter, and dark energy. Black hole and Big Bang intertwined. So, the size of the black hole equates to space-time—13.7 billion years, plus visible matter, plus dark matter, plus dark energy."

The audience stirred, a collective murmur intensifying as Joseph unfolded his revelation.

"Answer this, and we solve the enigma of information within a black hole. It's not lost; it transcends to another universe," he declared earnestly.

A seismic ripple of discussion reverberated through the crowd. Joseph, weary, leaned against the chalkboard.

"You're proposing the multiverse theory is true? Infinite universes coexisting in our cosmos?" inquired an old colleague, seeking confirmation.

Years passed in the span of Joseph's response, and his aged reflection in the audience's eyes deepened the gravity of his words. "Yes, that's my conviction."

Another colleague, still skeptical, asked, "And how do you intend to prove such a bold assertion?"

The weight of uncertainty hung in the air, but Joseph persevered, "I'm still formulating a method..."

Amidst the colleagues' deliberations, skepticism prevailed. "I thought this was a serious discussion?" scoffed one more colleague.

"It is," Joseph asserted, but a young colleague dismissed it is "science fiction, not science."

The room emptied as most colleagues exited, leaving Joseph to confront the solitude of his conviction. Time was unyielding, and Joseph aged before their eyes, becoming an older man.

The old colleague approached, offering a sober perspective. "Maybe it's time to relinquish this theory, Joseph. It's consumed your life. What has it brought you?"

"I know it's true," Joseph whispered, his gaze turned away in silent acknowledgment.

"It's a fanciful theory, Joseph. An older man's pursuit of an elusive dream. That's how they see you," his old friend remarked dismissively.

Joseph looked away, a silent acknowledgment of the internal struggle. "Thank you, but no thank you. I've dedicated my life to this, and I'll see it through," he declared with unwavering resolve.

The old friend shook his head, leaving Joseph in solitude. Joseph gazed at the empty room as the door closed, a silent witness to the echoes of his unwavering pursuit.

The lecture hall, suffused with intellectual tension, was momentarily disrupted as one of its doors swung open. Daisy, a woman in her early twenties, walked in, her eyes slightly confused as they scanned the room's occupants.

"Did I miss everything?" she inquired, breaking the lingering silence.

Having just faced a roomful of skeptical colleagues,

Joseph turned from the chalkboard, wiping away his equations. He offered a reassuring response.

"You didn't miss anything at all." Apologizing for being held up at work, Daisy approached her father, her youthful features contrasting with Joseph's weathered countenance.

"It's better that way. You've seen your father get ridiculed far too much," Joseph remarked. His weariness was evident.

Sensing the familiar struggle her father faced, Daisy inquired him. "That bad again?" she asked, concerned, creasing her brow.

Joseph, resigned but unwavering, replied, "The usual."

Daisy sighed, acknowledging the toll her father's relentless pursuit of a controversial theory had taken on him. She couldn't help but wonder about the cost of such unwavering dedication.

"Why continue to pursue this theory against so many detractors? Maybe it's time to admit that..."

Joseph cut her off with a firm declaration. "No. Never let anyone tell you what you have to do. If you believe in something, fight for it to the end."

Daisy, understanding her father's conviction, clarified her concern.

"I didn't mean it that way, Dad. You know I believe in you and your work, but even if you are right, with so many people working against you, how can you prove it?"

Resolute in his beliefs, Joseph spoke of a conviction that transcended external validation.

"One day, I will be proved right. I believe in this. I will keep trying and practicing my theory because, you know..."

But Daisy, interjecting with impatience, echoed the sentiment they both shared.

"Practice makes perfect. I know. (beat) We already know what needs to be done. Practice time is over."

Joseph acknowledged the truth in her words but emphasized the hurdles they faced.

"We know what needs to be done but need to know how. No known material can sustain the pressures of traveling through a black hole. If we find one, we can send a probe into it, collect data from inside, and hopefully do the same when it reaches the other side of wherever it's spit out."

However, Daisy had news to share progress in pursuing this seemingly impossible task.

The intrepid Daisy

Daisy was a small child when her father, Joseph, experienced his thought experiment while playing on a trampoline. Years after that faithful day, Daisy spent many hours alone with her thoughts.

She always wondered what would have happened if she had played on the swings or jungle bars. Would her dad have developed the same formula and had the same extraordinary life? One will never know, but one thing was true: she adored her father and would do anything to help him. As a result, her dad devoted his life to attempting to prove his theory. Most professionals in the science community rebuked his work, but it was not unnoticed by some people closest to him, including his daughter. So, it's not surprising how much he had influenced her. She saw how passionate Joseph was about the universe and how much work he put into everything the challenge presented. When any discussions about the project were whispered into Daisy's ear, she always gave herself a present. She spent countless hours in Joseph's lab learning anything to help her grow into an articulate person preparing for college.

When the time came for her to leave for college at sixteen, she went to the best engineering school in the United States, the Massachusetts Institute of Technology (MIT) in Cambridge, Massachusetts. As part of their engineering school, students can achieve specialty ranks in aerospace, aeronautical, and astronautical engineering (all ranked number one nationwide). MIT piqued Daisy's interest, and in the end, there was no question about which college her application would be mailed to MIT.

Daisy spent five years getting a Ph.D. in Aerospace Engineering. NASA recruited her out of school. After spending years at NASA working on various successful projects, they honored Daisy with the Associate

Administrator of Aeronautics Research appointment. Now, she was in a place to help her dad prove his theory.

Daisy looked forward to working with her dad. They were so close and spoke every day.

"Well, you'll be happy to know I'm searching for more materials."

Joseph, surprised by her continued dedication, questioned her testing endeavors.

"Are you still conducting tests?"

Daisy, undeterred, affirmed their shared goal.

"We want to prove your theory, don't we?"

Concerned about the practicalities and the support from a larger scientific community, Joseph inquired about NASA's involvement.

"But what is NASA saying? I'd assume they wouldn't want to waste the resources."

Daisy, with a sly smirk, reassured her father. "It's under the radar."

Joseph's concern deepened, but Daisy maintained her mischievous smile.

"Daisy..."

Her response held an air of defiance."(smirking) What? (beat) Even if your theory is wrong, you'd still be the first to create a probe that can penetrate a black hole. No one else can say that. I want to give you at least that victory."

Daisy knew it was time for her to become involved in the day-to-day practices of the project. Now, her attention would be on progressing the project to the end. She didn't want to act like politicians who support ventures only and never keep their promises.

Knowing something impressive needed to happen with this project, she met with the entire NASA aerospace research team. They decided the only way her dad's dream would stay alive would be to send a probe inside a black hole and collect the data from inside. As always, this was an impossible task. First, Sagittarius was thousands of light-years away, in the middle of the Milky Way Galaxy. More precisely, 26,000 light-years (a light-year is the distance a beam of light travels in a single Earth year). Second, a computer capable of sending information from inside the black hole back to NASA was necessary. No probe could enter a black hole without being destroyed by the immense gravity.

Daisy reached into her purse and placed a small spherical object on the desk in front of her dad. The sphere illuminated and broke apart with a button press, revealing a 3D projection of the probe's design—a long, thin, missile-like structure. Joseph looked at it in awe.

"You've come up with the design..."

"Yes, but I still need to figure out how to get it to travel 26,000 light-years to Sagittarius A, properly transmit the data, and most importantly, how to prevent it from breaking apart once it reaches the black hole," Daisy confirmed.

The moment of shared triumph was interrupted by Daisy's cell phone ringing. She swiftly put in an earpiece, taking the call.

"This is Daisy…"

Marlene's urgent voice on the other end signaled unforeseen developments.

"It's Marlene. You need to get back to base quick."

Daisy, her expression dropping in subtle shock, sought

clarification.

"What's going on?"

Marlene's voice conveyed urgency: "There's about to be an impact."

Daisy, processing the gravity of the situation, responded with a promise to be there. "I'll be right there."

Removing the earpiece, Daisy addressed her father. "Park yourself in front of a television, Dad. You're not

going to want to miss this."

With a kiss on Joseph's cheek, Daisy turned and briskly walked towards the exit, leaving Joseph with anticipation and a lingering question.

"Miss what?"

Daisy exited without answering, and the room, once filled with the weight of scientific pursuit, now resonated with the urgency of impending events, leaving Joseph pondering the impact that awaited them all.

3

The New Chapter begins

Joseph was getting old, and Daisy feared her dad would never see his theory proved. She had the design and concept for the probe, but she could not solve the three problems: distance, information, and resistance. But then, on the morning of August 15, 2071, a sudden opportunity was about to present itself and change the trajectory of Joseph's dream.

A year prior, Daisy and her team began detecting signs of an asteroid nearing the Milky Way Galaxy. Initially, calculations suggested the meteor would pass Earth at a safe distance. However, as it hurtled through space, its trajectory shifted, bringing it perilously close, within one-fourth the distance to the Moon. The team hastily revised their findings, revealing an alarming projection—the meteor was on a collision course with Earth, set to strike the Sahara Desert at a monstrous speed.

The NASA control room buzzed with a vibrant symphony of focused activity. Numerous screens flickered with intricate data, capturing the attention of dedicated employees engrossed in their tasks. Amidst this orchestrated chaos, a larger-than-life meteor glowed ominously on the central screen, its celestial trajectory a captivating spectacle.

31

Stepping into this dynamic tableau, Daisy, a seasoned figure in the room, fixed her gaze on Marlene. The young assistant was feverishly typing away at a computer, embodying a sense of urgency and purpose.

The room's hum lowered to a hushed murmur as Daisy approached Marlene, who turned to face her, a mix of concern and determination etched on her face.

Daisy's question cut through the ambient noise. "What the hell is going on?"

Marlene explained that the meteor had appeared unexpectedly, eluding any prior detection until a few hours ago. The ensuing discussion delved into the meteor's projected impact site and the feasibility of evacuation.

As the scientists waited for impact, they gave reports daily to ensure the public wouldn't panic. Knowing the meteor would hit Earth's atmosphere, the entire world focused their research on the meteorite on the planet.

Fortunately, the meteor was bound for an unpopulated area— the Sahara.

Daisy's gaze shifted to the mesmerizing trajectory displayed on the central screen, pondering the accuracy of satellite images capturing the celestial event.

The revelation prompted Daisy's reflection.

"I've never seen a meteor quite like that..."

Marlene concurred, emphasizing the unprecedented nature of the celestial intruder. The gravity of the situation lingered in the room.

A moment of profound realization passed through Daisy. "We need to get a team to the Sahara as soon as possible. If the Russians and Chinese beat us to the punch, we're screwed." With determination, Daisy turned and strode purposefully towards the exit, Marlene following in her wake. The conversation continued, addressing the approaching meteor's imminent contact and challenges.

"Get the Air Force involved. We need their blackbird jets. They'll get us there before impact."

Marlene, however, voiced concerns about potential repercussions, questioning the wisdom of being in the area when the meteor made contact.

"Get it done, Marlene. I want to be on a jet within the hour." With those resolute words, Daisy left the room, leaving Marlene behind. A heavy sigh escaped Marlene's lips as she contemplated the unknown challenges ahead in this celestial saga, a narrative unfolding against the backdrop of the vast Sahara and the impending celestial collision.

Three sleek Lockheed SR-71 Blackbirds were lined up on the runway, their powerful engines humming with anticipation. Daisy, flanked by a group of scientists, followed the pilots toward the jet fleet.

Inside the cockpit of one Blackbird, Daisy secured herself with practiced efficiency, adjusting her helmet and face mask. The pilot turned toward her, a wry smile on his face.

"You ready for this? It might be a bumpy ride."

Daisy answered (smirking), "I've been through worse. Let's get this show on the road."

As the pilot initiated takeoff procedures, the jet roared to life, accelerating with breathtaking speed. The G-forces pressed Daisy back into her seat.

After landing, Daisy unstrapped herself and said, "Well, that was something. Mind if I grab a barf bag?"

The pilot commented, chuckling, "Don't worry, you're not the first."

In the early morning, the Sahara Desert lay beneath a sky transitioning from darkness to hues of orange and pink. The approaching roar of a celestial collision became perceptible, heralding the meteor's descent. The flaming meteor crashed into the desert floor, unleashing a cataclysmic explosion that shook the Earth and cast a towering plume of sand and rock into the sky.

As the dust settled, a colossal crater emerged, deep into the Earth, with the meteor intact.

Several scientific teams and camps surrounded the crater, hazmat-clad scientists descending to extract samples. Standing at the crater's edge, Daisy observed with a furrowed brow.

The scientific community at the meteor's resilience and the unprecedented metal alloy it comprised is now known as Munerium.

The Munerium

A meteorite with an unknown origin, made of Munerium, impacted Earth.

When the Munerium meteorite fell in the middle of the Sahara Desert, it created a massive media rush and overwhelming fear among society. The media blew the entire incident out of proportion with their over-zealous reports on comets, meteorites, asteroids, and, don't forget, meteors. But the truth is the teams won the lotto with this meteorite.

Meteorites do not come from comets, which are more fragile than asteroids; ninety to ninety-five percent of meteors fizzle before reaching Earth's atmosphere. The Munerium meteorite beat the odds of being in the ten to five percent of making it through Earth's atmosphere without falling apart. As Munerium plummeted to Earth, it remained intact; not a single piece broke off. Something so important just dropped on the scientists' doorstep was, without a doubt, a miracle. People knew asteroids falling from the sky would break into several fragments because of the impact of Earth. However, if one were to measure the weight of an average asteroid falling from the sky, the weight would increase as gravity became a factor. This is because the Munerium did not break up.

Most scientists categorize meteorites into three

main types: stony, iron, and stony-iron, each with subgroups. Stony meteorites consist of minerals containing silicates, specifically silicon and oxygen. This extraordinary material of fantastic quality, which becomes even more potent when subjected to immense pressure and gravity, would be perfect for this project.

Munerium adapted to stress and outperformed any known substance on Earth. The behavior of the Munerium led the researchers to hypothesize that the atoms forming the material would transform into an indestructible crystalline structure. When tested under infinite pressure and gravity–not one buckle, distortion, or bend.

People believe the meteorite hitting Earth was a sign of the end of all times, but the reality of the impact was a miracle–a shot in the dark gift. Many people could not look past the asteroid's devastating impact; few believed it was an omen of worse things to come. Yet millions of people knew the beacon of light when they saw it, and these icons from industry: science, education, medicine, business, and so many more insisted the world would step up and help Earth get back on track.

When the meteorite hit, the National Security Administration's (NSA) scientists rushed to take control of all the information and analysis gathering. But after months of being no closer to a conclusion and overwhelmed by a plethora of data, the scientists were left with massive unanswered questions with no answers in sight. One of their first mistakes was not organizing teams, experts, and specialists to process the data dump. So, the first call they contacted was Daisy, the most notable meteoriticist in the world. One of her specialties known throughout the aerospace community was her work deciphering and identifying the compounds of stars, asteroids, comets, and meteors.

Daisy was passionate, as her road started years before, and she had to do this for her dad. Some tasks people embark on are enormous and maybe without optimism, especially if someone is trying to prove the hypothesis of a parent's lifelong dream. Daisy was not that person; she came from a family whose whole life was optimistic; regardless of the outcome, Daisy would always know she did the best she could.

Her first observation of the Munerium was that it never broke into pieces. The meteorite's strength must have a complex schematic, allowing it to resist the forces of atmospheric pressures.

Weeks later, transitioning to a NASA testing facility, Daisy and Marlene subjected a Munerium sample to intense gravity simulation. In recognizing its potential significance, Daisy expressed its critical role as the missing piece for interstellar travel. As the machine buzzed and the rock vibrated, it stabilized, eliciting shocked excitement from Marlene.

Daisy's laughter echoed in the testing facility as

she embraced Marlene, declaring triumphantly, "We have it! We have the missing piece!" The duo marveled at Munerium with a sense of accomplishment.

Now, she would need help to solve the other two puzzle questions – quantum computer and nuclear gravitational propulsion engine. She trusted the stars, knowing the answer would provide help soon.

Daisy had found her material and knew she was already looking into a future storm on the horizon, setting the stage for the next chapter in their quest for interstellar travel.

First, she needed to fabricate vast amounts of Munerium necessary to build a giant spaceship, so the teams worked to create a synthetic Munerium.

Then Daisy had an earth-shattering idea; she found a connection between the oxygen isotope inside Munerium and the Moon. The characteristics of the lunar oxygen isotopes comprise oxygen, silicon, magnesium, iron, calcium, and aluminum. Daisy calculated it would find the most potent isotopes in the dead volcanoes and craters. Would a synthetic Munerium be strong enough to withstand the crushing power of a black hole? The oxygen isotopes in rocks on the Moon may be identical or have features homogeneous to those on Earth. However, recent studies revealed the earthly and lunar oxygen isotopes were not as similar as thought. Although the isotopes may not be identical to the lunar isotopes, they will work well with the Munerium, making plenty for the spaceship. The chemical composition of the lunar rocks makes it possible for isotopes to withstand enormous amounts of pressure.

But now, the quest for raw materials and the intricate process of injecting oxygen isotopes into Munerium marked the next phase in her cosmic odyssey.

A new chapter had begun, and Daisy was determined to navigate the uncharted territories of science and space, propelled by the promise of interstellar travel and the unwavering optimism of her lineage.

Knight
Discoverer
from darkness
to light

4

2074: Pioneering the Future

While prodigious minds are busy with their inventions in 2074, the weather on Earth has reached a tipping point because of extreme deforestation and farming or construction on wetlands, to name just a few. The skeptics believed something was about to happen to the planet.

Coastal cities were being flooded, droughts were becoming more severe, storms had become more robust than ever, crises were being triggered in many countries, and millions were dying every year from the effects of climate change - The Runaway Greenhouse Effect. Scholars were not optimistic about the future of humanity on Earth. The weather patterns achieved positive feedback in a vicious cycle and became increasingly hostile to the world population. Everybody was looking toward the skies for a new possible, livable planet or Moon to sustain Earth's population.

Billions of years ago, Earth's twin, Venus, experienced the same destructive climate change as Earth. Harmful greenhouse gases like carbon dioxide destroyed Venus' atmosphere and caused its water bodies to evaporate, making it unbearable for life. The interior of Venus, made of a metallic iron core, comprises a molten rocky mantle. While on Earth, human activity and manufacturing industries killed the planet by releasing tremendous amounts of CO_2 into the atmosphere.

Earth continued to be ravished by climate change; coupled with human activity, Earth has sustained irreversible damage. Moreover, resources are dwindling at a faster rate, challenging the allocation to every person. This alone justifies the scientists' urgency for a breakthrough into another world.

Professors Heart and Christine were impressive scientists, and they were running against time to engage in a friendly competition to see which would have the most relevant invention of the decade.

Professor Christine was developing the first quantum computer. That device was based on the theory of quantum physics and quantum mechanics using the quantum entanglement property, which states that when two objects or particles are in contact, they remain connected forever, regardless of the distance. Therefore, the ability to connect information between unimaginable points in the universe or different universes would propel electronic technology far into the future.

Researchers put so much of their life into their projects. No one wants to put their name or reputation on the line only to fail. Then, a kernel of an idea explodes into the ultimate vision researchers have poured into their souls. That's what happened to Christine and Heart.

Professor Christine, a woman in her early 40s, was orchestrating a symphony of wires and equipment in her advanced lab. Running diagnostics on a Quantum Computer, she was typing with purpose, her eyes focused on the screen; she was in the latter stages of decoding, adjusting the last details of the motherboard to be operational.

Quantum entanglement brings forth a deeper understanding of the several worlds of quantum theory. Quantum entanglement is when quantum theory requires multiple worlds to exist or function. And when it happens, two worlds are not independent.

As the code ran through, the screen flashed a green light. Professor Christine, overwhelmed with astonishment, leans back in her chair. Cupping her mouth with her hands, she is on the verge of tears, realizing the monumental achievement. Developing this computer took decades; trial after trial frustrated the scientists until that day it showed promise. Finally, Christine's quantum computer opened the door to instant connections and information exchange between points in this universe and others.

In another cutting-edge facility, Professor Heart, in his late 40s, oversees a massive engine hanging from the ceiling. Scientists diligently worked around various ideas, contributing to the creation of a groundbreaking new type of propulsion.

Heart was typing notes into a computer, finalizing calculations with anticipation. He developed a new type of propulsion called the Ionic Nuclear Gravitation Engine (INGE). This new system would distort the space-time fabric and create a wormhole, serving as a shortcut through space-time. According to his calculations, he could reduce a journey of 1,000 light-years to less than an hour on Earth. As Einstein proposed in the past, "time is relative." A person traveling through space experiences a different passage of time and perspective than someone on Earth. This phenomenon arises due to gravity and Einstein's general theory of relativity. Gravity is a vital phenomenon representing everything with mass or energy pulled together or brought toward another. When someone jumps, gravity takes a person back down to the earth. When humans go to space, it's like tossing ashes into the air - they take time just flying above the surface as they have no significant weight.

When people travel in space, their experiences may differ because gravity is relative; time perception depends on the observer. Professor Heart had a straightforward explanation for his theory.

Imagine a sheet of paper, and there's a point in each extremity on that sheet of paper. Regular physics believes the smaller distance between two points is a straight line, but one could connect the two ends by bending the paper in half. Thus, creating a shortcut between two points in space by generating a wormhole;

he called this a space jump.

Therefore, it was imperative to have both Professor Christine's and Professor Heart's concepts proven so a suitable location for human colonization might begin. A glimmer of hope sparkled when both professors announced they had finished their missions and were ready to test them. First, however, both professors needed a spaceship strong enough to support the astronomical gravitational fluctuations involved in this experiment. The stage was set, and they now required the missing piece to bring their groundbreaking inventions to fruition.

Not having their vessel, the innovators contacted the one person who might help them, Daisy.

Knight
Discoverer
from darkness
to light

5

The Meeting:
The Confluence of Fates

Night hung heavy with inky darkness, tormented by an unrelenting storm. Rain, whipped by the hurricane-force winds, danced and twirled in the cyclone's fury. Lightning struck with determined frequency, illuminating the tumultuous scene while thunder resonated through the air.

Daisy's car wrestled against the elements, finding refuge in an empty space within the parking lot. The wind's pressure turned opening the car door into a formidable task. Undeterred, Daisy pressed forward toward the facility, gasping as lightning struck perilously close, revealing the ominous presence of three tornadoes in the distance.

Her steps quickened, propelled by the urgency to reach the facility's safety.

Inside NASA, within Daisy's office, Professors Christine and Heart, accompanied by Marlene, awaited Daisy's arrival. Drenched from the storm, Daisy entered the office with a surprised expression.

They had heard about her tests with Munerium and her thoughts on developing a space probe. So, when the professors called Daisy, she was ecstatic to hear about the prospect of testing Joseph's theory of black holes and alternative universes. But the professors had other ideas. They did not want to send a probe to Sagittarius; instead, they wanted to test the space jump and the quantum computer concepts to see if they would work. Daisy was adamant she needed to use the probe she designed after the first tests for Professors Heart and Cristina were successful.

Marlene attempted to convey that she had tried to call Daisy, and as Daisy acknowledged the presence of the Professors, they rose to greet her with handshakes.

The conversation unfolded, with Daisy recognizing the Professors for their significant contributions—Professor Christine for the quantum computer and Professor Heart for the space jump engine. Both Professors affirmed Daisy's observations, rising to greet her.

The moment's gravity became apparent as Daisy shared the completion of her prototype space probe using the Munerium material. The convergence of their projects held immense potential as they collectively realized the profound implications of their collaboration.

Amidst the urgency prompted by worsening global conditions—cities being swallowed by the oceans, drought, and catastrophic natural disasters—the Professors emphasized the critical need for Daisy's space probe to prove their theories. Daisy, in turn, highlighted the reciprocal reliance on each other's projects to validate her father's theory.

In contemplation, Daisy proposed a condition: the joint use of their projects for a second run, testing her father's theory. The Professors, after exchanging glances, reluctantly agreed.

Daisy's final offer, born of determination and a refusal to relinquish her pursuit, marked a pivotal moment in their collaboration. The Professors, nodding and sighing in acquiescence, acknowledged the gravity of the decision. With a broad smile, Daisy eagerly sealed the agreement with an enthusiastic handshake, setting the stage for the next chapter in their shared quest for humanity's survival.

This is how it should be in life - people embracing the power of negotiation. After all, life revolves around using what's at one's disposal. Scientists sought collaborative projects to benefit the masses; for a solution to saving Earth's inhabitants, all teams needed to stay united to the end.

With a compromise reached, everyone went on to create history about launching the engine computer probe, the trifecta team expected success. The scientists decided the first test would be in an empty Milky Way Galaxy, 1,000 light/years away from Earth. The probe should take only one hour in space-time but one year in Earth-time. When successfully tested, the probe will be sent out to make inquiries about the Sagittarius star.

They set a date for the test on September 22, 2075.

The Test

The long-awaited day had finally arrived. The teams watched as the rocket left the Earth, carrying the probe out of space. Daisy held her breath, waiting for any sign of trouble. Scrutinizing every part of the rocket for a deformation, bend, or buckle, then it happened. Without fanfare, the rocket released the probe. The Ionic Nuclear Graviton Engine was the first to fire and kick in, and the quantum computer began making calculations. But it was the probe that brought the most excitement when it created a distortion in the space-time fabric and formed a wormhole. Now, the probe will take one Earth year to transmit any data back to NASA. The only thing the team could do now was hope and pray the probe reached the correct location.

After the meeting, Daisy decided to see her father. In the quiet expanse of Joseph's home, the living room was aglow with the muted illumination of night. Seated on the couch, Joseph's eyes were fixed on the television screen, where a news broadcast unfolded. The rocket's image, ascending into the vast unknown, bore the headline "NASA Anxiously Awaits Data."

Daisy entered the room, cradling a cup of tea. She gently placed it on the coffee table before Joseph, acknowledging shared anticipation.

"Your big day is coming up," Joseph remarked.

"Our big day," Daisy responded, a soft smile accompanying her words. Joseph accepted the tea, sipping it with a weak smile.

"What do you think? In your bones... what are they telling you?" Joseph inquired.

Daisy's response carried a mixture of positivity and skepticism. Her colleagues, she noted, held optimism, yet she saw it as a veiled superstition. The odds, formidable adversaries, loomed against their ambitious endeavors.

"So did every scientist who tried to prove something into existence. You weren't the first, and you won't be the last,"

Joseph countered, attempting to infuse a note of reassurance. As the weighty conversation lingered, Daisy shifted the focus. "Enough about this. How are you doing? I know that the nurse called you."

"I'm fine," Joseph responded stoically. His nurse's recent call, tinted with negativity, was acknowledge but quickly brushed aside. Unintentionally serving as the nurse's confidant, Joseph navigated through the complexities of her struggles.

"At least you have someone to talk to daily," Daisy remarked, recognizing the silver lining.

"I'd rather her stay home and figure out her own life than worry about one that's about to expire," Joseph quipped, a sentiment of humor and resignation.

"Dad..." Daisy began, her concern evident.

Abruptly, a cough seized Joseph, its gurgling

intensity disrupting the room's serenity. Daisy, swift in her response, moved closer, inquiring about his well-being. Joseph, waving her concern away, discovered traces of blood on his hand and tried to hide the unsettling sight that followed. A handkerchief emerged, stained with crimson, tucked away as Daisy returned with a glass of water. Joseph, forcing a smile, dismissed the incident as a mere irritation in his throat.

Daisy's concern lingered, reflected in her gaze as it rested on the blood-stained handkerchief tucked away in Joseph's pocket.

6

A Tense Moment persists

In the vastness of space, the probe sailed effortlessly— an interstellar sojourner on its cosmic journey. A sudden activation of thrusters disrupted its tranquil trajectory, slowing it down almost to a standstill. The propulsion system glowed in a mesmerizing whitish-blue hue, expanding as it charged. The radiance intensified, creating an ethereal glow around the spacecraft. Without warning, the engine released a beam, piercing the cosmic void until it encountered an unseen barrier, halting its progress.

As if nature yielded, a surreal opening materialized—a hole in the fabric of space and time. A breathtaking swirl of colors danced within this newfound passage—an otherworldly spectacle defying cosmic laws.

Responding to the cosmic call, the probe engaged its thrusters, propelling itself towards the enigmatic wormhole. As the spacecraft entered the celestial tunnel, flashes of light enveloped it, creating a kaleidoscope of luminescence. The cosmic gateway swallowed the probe in a seamless transition, leaving only an eerie silence.

One year mark of the launch arrived. Everyone

from the teams gathered in mission control, awaiting any sign of life. After a day of waiting, there was only silence and a murmur of sad voices. Again, instead of the control room silence throughout mission control, there is still no sound of "computer life."

In the control room, Daisy, Professor Christine, Professor Heart, and Marlene anxiously observed screens displaying incoming data. Various scientists hurriedly moved about, checking different computers in a symphony of focused chaos. Professor Christine, frustration etched across her face, voiced her impatience, "We should've gotten data back from the probe hours ago."

Daisy, the voice of reason, responded calmly, "Give it time. There are no rules to this."

Sharing Christine's concern, Professor Heart added, "I have to agree with Professor Christine here. If we don't get data soon, it's safe to say the mission failed." The optimist Marlene interjected, "Don't jump the gun. If Daisy says we're fine, then we're fine." Daisy acknowledged Marlene's support with an encouraging smile.

Thomas, a man in his early 40s wearing NASA attire, approached. Daisy turned to him, intrigued. "Excuse me for interrupting," Thomas said. Daisy looked at him, and he continued, "Have we received any data yet?"

Marlene, with a touch of sarcasm, replied, "Trust me... you would know."

Thomas, realizing the gravity of the situation, expressed surprise and concern, "Oh..."

Daisy reassured him, "This place would go bonkers if we did."

On a mission from the Commander, Thomas added, "I apologize. The Commander sent me to gain any intel..."

The tension in the room lingered, and the uncertainty of the mission hung heavily in the air.

"You can tell your Commander he shouldn't hold his breath," Professor Christine sarcastically said.

Sensing the tension, Thomas asked, "Is there an issue?" "Not that we know of...yet. Perhaps the probe wasn't strong enough," Professor Heart added.

Marlene, with a hint of skepticism, threw in her thoughts, "Or maybe your quantum computer shits the bed. Or your space jump engine failed."

Daisy intervened, trying to diffuse the situation, "Marlene... it's fine." The professors walked off with irritated gazes, but Daisy and Marlene shared a lighthearted moment before following suit.

Thomas cleared his throat and extended his hand, introducing himself, "I'm Thomas, by the way."

Daisy shook his hand and began introducing herself, but Thomas said, "I know who you are. It's an honor to meet you, Daisy." She was taken aback, and she couldn't help but smile. "So... I assume you believe this will eventually succeed?" Thomas continued.

"I do. I know it will." Daisy affirmed confidently,

Thomas nodded, "Then, in that case... I know it will as well." They shared a moment, exchanging slight smiles. Thomas stepped back, concluding, "Pleasure meeting you," and walked away.

Marlene marked time by crossing off a day on her calendar. Nine X's now occupied the space where the one-year mark was circled. She sighed, glancing at Daisy, who stood in the center of the room, holding a cup of coffee, visibly exhausted.

Seated near the front, Professors Christine and Heart wear expressions of irritation.

"All those years... wasted," Professor Christine said, frustrated.

Professor Heart says, "Our work is trial and error..."

"We didn't have the time for trial and error," Christine retorts.

Marlene walks up to Daisy with concern in her eyes. Waiting over the past year was the most stressful for all the team members. They had no proof that the probe survived; did it disintegrate as soon as it entered the wormhole?

The longer the silence loomed, the more nervous everybody became, but Professor Christine broke the silence, "We will hear news from the probe, and we will be successful. We should receive data from the probe within the next few hours."

They waited and waited - hours became days, and days became weeks until weeks became a month.

Dismayed, Professors Christine and Heart did not know what happened. Maybe the probe was not strong enough, the quantum computer did not work, or the space jump was unsuccessful. They questioned every aspect of their projects and mission. Yet, Daisy would not admit defeat, knowing what she had built. Instead, she said, "I know it will work, no doubt at all." She had developed this patience from the years she started her father's groundbreaking theory.

Putting all one's faith in a probe took gumption, yet good news will always prevail; all one needs to do is believe. Just at the point of no return and complete failure emerged the sound everybody has been waiting to hear–printers buzzing, monitor screens turning on, and the sigh of relief from the trifecta team.

Suddenly, a transmission feed appeared on the main screen, capturing everyone's attention. The room fell silent in anticipation. Marlene took Daisy's arm as data was streamed across every computer screen and the main display. The room erupted in joy. Finally, after thirty-two days of waiting, the quantum computer sent a signal saying the ship had reached the destination and all the instruments were working well and in perfect condition. The mission control room exploded in celebration when seeing this news. They had pulled it off — they had pulled the impossible off.

"We did it! You did it, Daisy!" Marlene exclaims.

Daisy rushed to the nearest computer, typing

frantically. Initially in awe, now Professor Christine and Professor Heart shared a moment of joyous celebration. They laugh, embracing each other as the weight of success lifts the frustration that had lingered for so long. The room is now filled with the triumphant energy of achievement.

Daisy's eyes move frantically back and forth as she processes the incoming data. "The probe reached its destination... all the instruments are still in full working order," she announces with disbelief and joy. After a brief pause, she adds, "It's a success. It went through the wormhole..."

She stands, her gaze sweeping across the room with shock. Amid her astonishment, Thomas approaches and embraces her. The two share a brief moment before pulling away.

Daisy, feeling a bit embarrassed, looks away with a shy smile. The connection between the two of them was apparent from the beginning.

She turned her attention back to the main screen. Besides that, one embrace with Thomas was as much as Daisy would celebrate. This was indeed a success, but only step one. Now, she finally had the chance to prove her father was right. The room was filled with relief and anticipation as to when they would embark on the next phase of their mission.

Professors Christine and Heart could not contain themselves, but Daisy was quite pleased by the news but still unsatisfied. Instead, her thoughts were with

Joseph. How much he endured, how much ridicule and mockery thought to be the laughingstock of the scientific community. He told the world about the possibilities of black holes and the big bangs; now she can prove that everything her father communicated to them was right – she will not squander this opportunity.

Knight
Discoverer
from darkness
to light

7

The Work in progress

In the NASA testing facility, dozens of scientists diligently worked on building two probes resembling the first.

Daisy inspects their progress with a furrowed brow.

Munerium, the material the meteor was made of, was a miracle material that came from the heavens and gave hope to save humankind. The only problem was they were running out of material. They had just enough to create two more test probes to go through the black hole, but after that, very little to work with.

Marlene conducted tests on a piece of Munerium and a Moon rock, discovering a connection between the oxygen isotopes. A message on her computer screen flashes "Match." Standing before the main screen, Marlene discusses her findings with Daisy, Professor Christine, and Professor Heart. "So, you see... I think our Moon and that meteor were the same. Maybe at the formation of Earth, this giant rock came colliding with us, and pieces broke off. One was big enough to form the Moon and trapped within our orbit. Other pieces, like the one that fell in the Sahara, floated off," Marlene explained. "So, do you think this meteor had been floating around for 4.5 billion years and then finally decided to come back?" Professor Christine answered.

Marlene confidently asserted, "I know that's what happened." And she turned to the screen, showing an image of the Moon. "For these two probes to work, it will be necessary to have enough Munerium from the Moon to build a large ship to house people."

"That's if we're successful. A very big if." Professor Heart expresses doubt.

Daisy intervenes, stating, "There are no more ifs, Professor.

We know what we need to do."

Professor Heart is concerned with the differences between a black hole and a wormhole. Daisy reassures, "There's no need for patronizing. I'm aware of that. We already know that Munerium can withstand the pressures of the gravity of a black hole. Now, it all depends on our final design."

So, she reveals Marlene's design for drones to explore the new universe and find a suitable planet. The catch was that each drone needed an ionic engine and quantum computer.

Half of the space drones must be available and operational for deploying and exploring this alternative universe. This was important because the drones would search for a habitable planet.

Professor Christine asked about the number of drones, to which Daisy responded, "Two hundred each, so four hundred total."

The professors expressed worry about the workforce requirement. Daisy asserts, "We have all the resources you need. Humanity is at stake. Every country is joining NASA in this effort. It may take some time, but we must be patient."

Marlene adds, "Patient is an understatement."

Professor Christine questions the reason and Marlene reveals, "By our calculations, it could take up to twenty-six years for us to know if the probes made it through."

"Twenty-six years?!" Professor Heart reacts.

"Twenty-six hours in space-time... twenty-six years for us on Earth." Daisy clarified.

And Marlene concluded, "That means getting started. The faster we get these probes to Sagittarius A, the faster we begin our twenty-six-year countdown."

The Professors exchange glances and quickly leave the room. Daisy snickered, and Marlene gave her a wink before walking off, leaving Daisy to reflect on the challenges ahead.

Finally, the Allen and Carr probes, named by Daisy, were ready with the drones installed. Everything was ok for the historic launch.

At the NASA launch site during the day, Daisy, Marlene, Professor Christine, Professor Heart, and Thomas stand in the distance. They watched with anticipation and hope as the two probes were launched into space.

The actual waiting game had begun, marking the

beginning of a prolonged period of uncertainty as they awaited the outcome of their ambitious mission.

Days later, in a medical center, Daisy and Joseph sit in front of a doctor reviewing some charts.

Joseph, resigned to the truth, urges the doctor, "There's no need to beat around the bush. Just tell me how it is."

The doctor, putting down the charts, delivers the news, "It's progressing."

"What does that mean?" concerned, Daisy asks

Joseph, acknowledging the reality, "It means my time is up."

The doctor offers a glimmer of hope, "Well, not necessarily. Considering what stage you're at, you do qualify for a new drug on the market. In most cases, you would be completely cured."

Joseph, skeptical, questions, "And the others? What kind of horrible side effects would I have?"

The doctor delivers a grim truth, "Just one. Death."

Joseph snickers and declines the offer, "Thanks, but no thanks."

Daisy, not ready to give up, interjects, "Wait..."

Joseph looks at Daisy curiously as she requests a moment with the doctor.

After she returned the doctor's office, Daisy tried to convince Joseph, "Dad... you're still young. We just launched the probes..." Facing the harsh reality, Joseph challenges her optimism, "You think I'll still be around in twenty-six years?"

Daisy responds with conviction, "Yes..."

Joseph notes her change in tone, "That's the first time you haven't sounded positive about an answer."

Daisy suggests that he will take that new drug, but Joseph is hesitant, "If I try it and die, what good does that do any of us?"

"If you don't try it, you'll still die, which won't do us any good either." Frustrated, Daisy expresses her dedication to Joseph's theory and pleads with him, "I've dedicated my life to your theory. The least you can do is try and extend yours to see it through."

After contemplating, Joseph sighs and reluctantly agrees, "Okay."

Daisy smiles and embraces him, relieved that he will give the new drug a chance.

Fortunately, Joseph was one of the lucky ones who saw his disease disappear completely. Now, he and the rest could join in on the waiting game.

Thirteen years later

Daisy is peacefully asleep in her bed. Suddenly, her cell phone rings, jolting her awake.

She rubs her eyes in sleepiness and reaches for her nightstand, grabbing her earpiece and putting it in.

Daisy answers, still half-asleep, "Hello...?"

Marlene's voice on the phone demands urgency,

"You need to come to the control center as soon as possible."

Now fully awake, Daisy furrows her brow and sits up, asking, "Why? What happened?"

Marlene's urgency is evident, "Allen... it started transmitting data."

Realizing the implications, Daisy expresses disbelief, "That's impossible. The probes shouldn't be able to transmit data inside the wormhole... Unless it came out..."

Marlene cuts in, insisting, "Just get here, Daisy."

She ended the call and, with a sense of urgency, she quickly got up, preparing to face the unexpected situation at the control center.

In NASA's Mission Control, Daisy and Marlene scrutinize the data displayed on the screens.

Daisy analyzes the readings, noting, "These readings are coming from the center of the Milky Way..."

Marlene explained, "Allen's ionic engine failed halfway through its journey. The engine ventilation system overheated and stopped working. It triggered the Quantum computer to start transmitting."

Daisy, overcome with frustration, exclaims, "Shit! All of those drones..."

Marlene, attempting to console her, places a hand on Daisy's shoulder, saying, "We still have Carr. It's exactly why we built two."

Daisy, filled with apprehension, reflects, "Yeah...

but now I have to spend the next thirteen years ripping my hair out. If Carr fails..."

Marlene reassures her, "It's not going to fail."

Daisy nods, looking up towards the screens, grappling with the uncertainty ahead in continuing their mission.

In the control room, the air is filled with tension. It's been thirteen years since Allen failed, and the time has come to renew Earth's hopes while waiting for news from the Carr probe. The atmosphere is calm, all eyes fixated on the screens, eagerly awaiting crucial data. Daisy stands near the back of the room, accompanied by Marlene, who is seated. Professors Christine and Heart are sitting near the front, their expressions stoic.

Marlene breaks the silence with a lighthearted comment, "I don't think you've sat for eight straight hours, Daisy."

"I can't."

Marlene chuckled and turned her attention back to the screen, expressing her exhaustion, "I think if I stare at this screen a second longer, my eyes are going to melt out of my head."

Suddenly, a line of data scrolls across the screen. Daisy gasps, and the room falls into a collective hush. Then, a slew of data pours in, and the room erupts in celebration.

"It made it! It made it!" Marlene exclaims.

While still focused on the data, Daisy reveals, "It's

just outside Sagittarius A..."

Professors Christine and Heart make their way over, shaking hands with Marlene and then Daisy.

"This is it. All those years... I hope it wasn't for nothing."

Professor Christine reflects with hope

Daisy reassures them, "It won't be."

"How much longer?" Professor Heart inquired about the timeline.

"Just a few more hours... maybe a day. It's approaching the black hole as we speak." The room is charged with anticipation and hope as they inch closer to the culmination of their long journey.

She continues, "Once it stops transmitting data... that's when we'll know it's entered. If it goes through... the data will start up again."

She takes a step back, inhaling deeply, as the critical moment approaches. The room remains on edge, collectively holding their breath, awaiting the outcome of the Carr probe's encounter with the black hole.

In the vast expanse of space near Sagittarius A, the Carr probe approaches the ominous mouth of the black hole. The golden light swirls around it as the probe is irresistibly drawn into the darkness.

As the probe enters the black hole, the tremendous gravitational forces at play compress its body to half its original size, stretching it to four times its size. The probe undergoes a surreal transformation.

Then, in an instant, it's gone. The void of the black hole absorbs the Carr probe, leaving a sense of mystery and awe in the cosmic abyss. The room remains tense as they wait for any sign of the probe's status.

Days and days passed with no signs of a transmission. Daisy felt destroyed; everything the teams worked so hard to may come to invent nothing, as well as the proof of her dad's theory. In her head, her dad says, "Rise, keep your head in the game. I have given you the ability to always feel hope and faith. I never taught you to quit; don't start now." She perked up, deciding to check in at mission control. Walking in, she noticed an indicator light blinking on the monitor; she stopped breathing momentarily. Carr was transmitting.

Carr was sending info from an alternative universe. Tears streamed down her face; she then knew her dad had always been right. He was right.

Daisy started running diagnostics; it had survived, damaged but intact. Half of the space drones were available and operational for deploying and exploring this alternative universe. This was important because the drones would search this new universe for a habitable planet. Working with Professor Christine and Professor Heart was a joy that filled Daisy's heart. It was a day to remember, all the team's hard work to prove her father's theory. She found the answers.

Knight
Discoverer
from darkness
to light

8

A Farewell

Daisy burst into her father's house, a swirl of triumph and closure enveloping her. Yet, the joyous moment swiftly transformed into a nightmare as she found Joseph lying on the floor, breathless, teetering on the edge of death. Hastily, she dialed for an ambulance and began CPR. After an agonizing eternity, a pulse finally responded. The paramedics arrived, initiating life support procedures.

As she drove to the hospital, disbelief gripped her. The triumphant celebration had turned into a devastating reality; her vibrant father now lay in critical condition. In the emergency room, Daisy watched the doctors desperately working to stabilize him. All she yearned for was a moment alone with him to share the incredible results that validated his life's work.

Eventually granted permission to speak to her father, Daisy saw the frailty in his weakened state. The elation of their success clashed with the harsh truth of his imminent departure. A man who had relentlessly pursued his theory now faced mortality.

Watching a once lively parent succumb to sickness is a painful experience. The body may fail, but glimpses of their vibrant past linger in their eyes.

Daisy and her father wept, realizing this conversation marked their final exchange. Amidst the celebration, Joseph confronted death. However, hearing that his groundbreaking theory would reshape space travel brought a measure of solace.

Daisy said to her dad, "You were right, Papa. All this time, you were right. You made the biggest discovery of the century. Your theory will go down in the history books as the greatest achievement of ALL time!" Mustering the quietest whisper, he said "You, my beloved daughter, are my greatest achievement. What you became will be my legacy."

Daisy sensed he needed to know nothing would have been achieved had it not been for his initial work all those years back. She also told him that whatever career she would have later in her life was because of Joseph's ideas and work. Of course, Joseph wanted to give Daisy all the credit, but it was his to relish.

A smile broke his face after Daisy's speech about how the project was all his work; delighted, she smiled back. As for Joseph, he looked sideways as the smile on his face broke into a concerned countenance.

He knew his time had come. He struggled to look at his daughter, knowing their celebration was over; Daisy knew, too. In the end, his heart gave out before his love for life. He looked back at her and said, "Please take the hourglass and this necklace with the crucifix." Daisy's world started spinning around her; she felt her heart freezing.

"Don't leave me alone. I can't do this without you," said Daisy between her sobs. Right before he passed, he heard his daughter's sad words. He looked up, smiled, and blew her a kiss, his way of saying, "You'll be fine." Daisy would have to believe her dad and know she can never be alone with her father's love inside her soul. Sadly, Daisy sat beside him as tears trickled down her cheeks with no words coming out of her mouth. After some time, she burst out crying, and it came out so uncontrollably, and she was inconsolable.

An extravagant burial ceremony honored Joseph Silva, an exceptional individual, exalting his kind, optimistic, and faithful life. Finally, the mourners celebrated his life's work and diligent sacrifice to save the Earth. The celebration continued well into the night; everybody knew his absence would profoundly affect their lives, but many of the people celebrating his life were project team members, and they understood the effort they were making would go into the history books in his honor.

Knight
Discoverer
from darkness
to light

9

A New Beginning

Daisy, burdened by grief, stood watchfully over scientists engrossed in testing equipment. The room buzzed with activity, yet her mind lingered on the solemn moments at her father's bedside.

Throwing herself back into the Knight Discoverer project, Daisy worked tirelessly, hoping for a breakthrough from one of the space drones sent through the black hole by Carr. Time was of the essence, and the fate of humanity hung in the balance. Working day and night, Daisy had never allowed herself the luxury of personal relationships. However, the passing of her father left her emotionally frail, leading her to seek guidance from a psychiatrist to navigate the unresolved emotions tied to her father's legacy.

Gradually, Daisy found solace and began reclaiming her sense of self. Her focus returned to the meticulous work of scientists and engineers, surrounded by the rhythmic hum of machinery. The room in NASA's Mission Control was dimly lit, with Daisy seated at a desk cluttered with coffee cups, evidence of her prolonged vigil.

A blueprint of the Knight Discoverer spaceship lay before Daisy, symbolizing their aspirations. As they awaited intel from Carr's drones regarding a possible habitable planet in the new universe, the urgency to build a spaceship capable of safely traversing the black hole grew.

Daisy's gaze shifted to the Moon, where abundant Munerium awaited their endeavor. Beyond Earth, her vision saw the construction of the spaceship on the Moon itself, utilizing the available resources to ensure humanity's survival.

In the quiet intensity of the testing facility, Daisy stood at the nexus of grief and determination, navigating the path forward for humanity. The legacy of her father's pioneering spirit lived on in her relentless pursuit of the unknown.

Marlene, sensing Daisy's fatigue, approached with concern. "Why don't you go home and get some rest? You've been here for two days straight," Marlene suggested.

Daisy shook her head, unable to tear away from the screens. "Not until I know. I can't."

Thomas, now a middle-aged confidant and lover, entered the room. Marlene, intercepting him, urged, "Try to get her to go home."

"Easier said than done," Thomas replied, glancing at Daisy. Marlene insisted, "If she won't listen to me, she'll listen to you."

With a smirk, Thomas approached Daisy, suggesting, "Maybe you should switch to espressos?" Daisy, startled, turned to him. "I thought you were busy?" "To miss you being introduced as the savior of the world? I wouldn't miss it," Thomas replied. Daisy's response was tinged with self-doubt. "Don't get too excited. I may have failed the whole world."

"Even if this test fails, you didn't fail anything. At least you tried. No one else can say otherwise," Thomas reassured her. A small smile formed on Daisy's lips as she grabbed Thomas' hand. They interlocked fingers, both fixating on the screens. Marlene, noticing the connection, smirked before focusing on her tasks.

As the tension in the room heightened, a beeping noise resonated. Daisy swiftly turned her head to the main screen. Moments later, data poured in, filling the screen with crucial information.

Daisy gasped, and a wave of cheers erupted from the scientists. Marlene rushed over to Daisy, embracing her tightly, tears streaming down their faces. "We did it... we did it," Daisy whispered in awe.

Thomas, equally captivated, stepped forward, examining the data. "This is... unbelievable. It's a new universe."

He turned back to Daisy. "Your Dad was right. You were both right."

Eager to share the news, Marlene hurried to a computer and started typing. "The drones were released. They're starting their exploration!"

Concern crossed Daisy's face as she inquired, "How many made it?"

Marlene's response held a tinge of disappointment.

"Looks like... just about half. I'm not getting readings from the others. They must have been damaged or destroyed in the process."

Worry etched itself on Daisy's features. Thomas, quick to offer comfort, moved closer, holding her hands. "No frowning today. You just discovered everyone's lifetime put together. You saved humanity," Thomas reassured her.

Daisy acknowledged, "Almost... it's up to those drones to find a new inhabitable planet. Then we can say we saved humanity." Thomas emphasized, "But this is the biggest victory of all. Celebrate it."

Daisy pondered for a moment, then nodded with a slight smile. Suddenly, her eyes widened. Daisy looked back at Thomas, who nodded with a supportive smile. She turned and hurried away.

Marlene couldn't resist a playful remark. "Would you two get a room already?"

Thomas, feigning innocence, replied, "I'm not sure what you're..."

Marlene interrupted with a knowing smirk. "Save it, Thomas. A woman always knows all."

Meanwhile, Daisy and Thomas shared a moment of connection as they walked down a hallway, discussing the absence of someone dear to them. Despite the emotional exchange, the atmosphere turned lighthearted as they navigated a power outage, finding humor in the darkness.

Amid laughter and playful banter, Thomas and

Daisy ended up in a meeting room, where their connection deepened into a passionate kiss. The scene transitioned to a more intimate moment as they undressed and shared a tender embrace on the floor. In the aftermath, lying curled up together, Thomas broached a personal topic about family and commitment.

He questioned Daisy's perspective on starting a family, prompting a reflective conversation about her motivations and priorities. The discussion turned unexpectedly when Thomas revealed a hidden ring, expressing his desire to marry Daisy.

Overwhelmed with emotion, Daisy accepted the proposal, and they shared a tender moment before the lights came back on.

As they quickly gathered their clothes and got dressed, the atmosphere was filled with laughter and joy, marking a significant moment of connection and commitment for the couple.

Knight
Discoverer
from darkness
to light

10

A New Horizon

Daisy remained immersed in designing the Knight Discoverer while eagerly awaiting any information from the space drones released by Carr. Tension escalated as the realization set in that the entire project might be in vain.

For the past two weeks, Daisy hadn't been feeling well, grappling with lethargy and occasional nausea. Concerned, Thomas urged her to seek medical advice. Together, they visited a medical office at NASA, where Daisy underwent an examination and blood work. The atmosphere changed when the doctor entered with a reassuring smile, delivering unexpected news: "You're pregnant!"

Daisy and Thomas stared at her, a mix of surprise and joy washing over them. Then, finally, she spoke, "I cannot believe this; how did this happen?!"

The doctor tilted her head to Daisy, "I think you know the answer to that question."

Shocked but overjoyed, Thomas looked at Daisy and declared, "This is a wonderful surprise. But, of course, getting married to you is number one, too."

Mixed emotions overwhelmed Daisy—happiness for continuing her family legacy but also anxiety about bringing a child into a troubled world.

With these conflicting emotions, Thomas and Daisy left the medical office, stunned yet ecstatic, knowing their love had created a human being just for them.

Despite the joy, Daisy recognized the urgency for the space drones to make contact; otherwise, her contribution to a new life might be overshadowed by the looming extinction of humanity.

Startled by her phone ringing, Thomas answered, "Hello?" "Daisy?" said Marlene, her assistant. "Hold on, she's right here," he handed Daisy the phone, as she quietly said, "What's up, Marlene?"

"What's wrong? Something's wrong. Are you okay? Did the doctor give you some bad news?"

Daisy looked at Thomas to see if he thought telling Marlene about the baby would be okay. He smiled and nodded, "Yes."

"No, there's no bad news, only good news–no–spectacular news. I am pregnant. Thomas and I just came out of the doctor's office. I will have a child."

Marlene started screaming and exclaimed, "I am so happy for you! Congrats! This couldn't have happened on a better day." "What? What's happened? Why did you call me?" Daisy said with concern.

Marlene excitedly replied, "I will tell you the news is unbelievable. You're just not going to believe it."

Daisy, curious and confused with the conversation, replied, "What?????? Tell me."

Marlene settled down and said, "Are you sitting and calm?

This is HUUUUUUUUUUUUUUUGE!"

"I am in my car, so yes, I am sitting. Tell me already!" Daisy replied.

Marlene exclaimed, "We found it! We found it!"

Daisy, caught between anticipation and bewilderment, responded, "Found what????????????"

Marlene started crying. Filled with excitement and emotion simultaneously, she replied, "One of the space drones started transmitting data from a solar system. This is a dual solar system; one planet is in the habitable zone and has an atmosphere and gases like Earth and liquid water on its surface! So, we found Earth 2.0.!"

Daisy and Thomas started hugging, and then Daisy cried. A ton of weight on her shoulders floated away after carrying it around for thirty years; her teams had accomplished the impossible. Marlene, still on the phone, was screaming and crying with happiness.

New Earth, a new beginning for humanity. Another miracle. Daisy, still hugging Thomas, calmed down and replied, "This morning, I had no hope for our child's future, and now there's nothing to hold our child back. Thank you, Lord. You are a miracle worker." They named the new Earth Canaan and the two stars orbiting Canaan, AFDATA, and JSA.

So, the only logical next step was a trip to the Moon and constructing a lunar base for isotope collections. Although the Moon lunar base construction was not quick, the team had all the information required, including the tools to be used. Daisy received daily reports on the station's development. Working at NASA was a great asset, making monitoring progress easier. Ultimately, the completed base started sending isotopes to Daisy's lab. With the production line regularly collecting and shipping back isotopes, Daisy could embark on the next step.

11

Alexander

Amidst the whirlwind of work, Daisy found it challenging to fully embrace the moments of pregnancy. Yet, when she managed to steal precious moments, they became extraordinary. Rocking gently in a chair, Thomas drove to Vermont to acquire a unique artisan creation he had long admired. Daisy's hopes and joys became intertwined with the round belly she affectionately rubbed. During their first ultrasound, tears welled in Daisy's eyes—this child was a miracle destined to conquer the world. Each check-up with Thomas brought overwhelming awe at witnessing the growth and the heartbeat of life inside her.

One restless night, contractions began. Planning to wake Thomas when they intensified, she drifted into a brief sleep, only to be awakened by an unexpected jolt of pain.

In agony, Daisy's focus shifted to the dawn, signaling the first light to the world. "Thomas, Thomas... I think I'm having a contraction. The pain won't go away," she managed to express.

Following the ambulance to the hospital, Thomas entered a chaotic E.R. A team prepared Daisy for surgery while a nurse guided him to the waiting room, collecting medical information. Anxiety etched on his face; Thomas sought answers. "What's wrong? What's going on?"

"She has a tear in the amniotic sac, and the doctors are going to do a cesarean section immediately," the nurse explained.

"Can I see her? I can't have anything happen to the two of them," Thomas implored, teetering on the verge of tears. "Of course. We need to get you gowned so you can see your new baby. Let's go quickly; the baby is not going to wait," the nurse said with a smile on her face.

In the surgical room, Daisy rejoined Thomas, appearing exhausted and scared yet filled with excitement. The words, "Okay, Dad, it's about time to see your new baby," signaled a moment of exhilaration. Behind a screen, Thomas witnessed the birth, a profound and unforgettable experience. He cut the umbilical cord and welcomed a baby boy.

The doctors continued working on Daisy to ensure the rupture was resolved and there was no additional damage. The baby was quickly attended to for the necessary medical attention.

The joyous moment took a sudden turn when Alexander's cry didn't ring out immediately. Panic set in as Thomas watched C.P.R. being administered. In an instant, the sweet sound of a wail filled the room. Thomas rushed back to Daisy, cradling their newborn son, Alexander.

The Young Alexander

Raised in the Christian faith, Alexander, along with his parents, faithfully attended church every weekend, finding solace and tradition in their familial bond amidst the challenges of overseeing a monumental project and raising a family.

In the serene ambiance of a crowded church, worshippers sang hymns led by a Reverend, their collective voices echoing through the sacred space. Thomas, Daisy, and a young Alexander harmonized with the congregation in song.

Post-church family meals had became a tradition. In the tranquil setting of Daisy's home, the dining room served as a hub of familial connection. Daisy, Thomas, and young Alexander gathered around the table, sharing a meal and engaging in meaningful conversation.

Meanwhile, Daisy juggled overseeing the Knight Discoverer and raising her son. In their conversations, Daisy shared memories of her youth, recalling her father's black hole theory and the challenges accompanying its development. Thomas praised Daisy's achievements, emphasizing her role in proving the theory.

Intrigued, Young Alexander expressed a desire to contribute to building the spaceship, prompting laughter from Daisy and Thomas. Embracing her son's aspirations, Daisy assured him he would join the team when he was older. However, Alexander's plea to help immediately revealed the challenges he faced at school due to the family's unconventional endeavors.

Daisy offered wisdom, emphasizing the importance of faith and perseverance in the face of skepticism. She handed Young Alexander a crucifix, a cherished symbol of her father's legacy, encouraging him to trust his intuition as a connection to God's guidance.

In a poignant moment, Young Alexander stood outside Daisy's home, clutching the crucifix, and prayed for wisdom in facing the challenges ahead. The horizon revealed an approaching storm, symbolizing the uncertainties that lay on their journey.

Daisy and Thomas cherished their son to grow up with love and support. He was adored, and they spent all their time with him. Their attention paid off; Alexander became a curious and quizzical child.

He loved spending his spare time at NASA with his mom and dad. Like his mother, who was also a "lab rat" when she was young, he just couldn't stay away. He observed his parents working on pieces of the shuttle, analyzing data, and sitting in on meetings now and then. Eventually, he knew he would become an astronaut, dazzled and dismayed by this career forever.

Within himself, he felt the responsibility of one day taking charge of many people's lives. With that burden weighing on him at such an early age, he always turned to the Lord for guidance, foreshadowing the challenges that awaited him on the path to fulfilling his destiny.

On his tenth birthday, Daisy gave him the Silva legacy, an hourglass with the inscription, "Time is Relative. Brilliance was Not. From Darkness into Light," it became an anthem to the character of everyone in the family.

Never forgetting, she created a gold bracelet with the family motto, "God's Blessing and Hard Work," entrusting Alexander to uphold the values, ideals, and determination given to her by both his parents. Many people in the aeronautics field knew his family well and would have been more than happy to give him the upper hand, but he had always worked hard. Alexander's track to success may have been paved by the difficult times of his grandfather and mom, but Alex could not rest on his laurels.

Joseph started his dream with no more than one idea, a concept with few believers and barely any resources or people to help. Alexander hated it when his mother told him how people ridiculed his granddad, saying his ideas would never be proven. For him, it sounded like it was just yesterday, and he felt it was his responsibility to work harder to keep proving to people how far someone would go to achieve their dream.

On many occasions, when his parents would work

late, they would come home and find him in the kitchen cooking. If mom seemed too tired, he would also do the dishes. His family was all about having each other's back, and he did not take this lightly; he would continue to support his future children in the same way. Plus, he would always seek guidance from the Lord.

The years swiftly passed; he was on track to graduate from high school early, just like his mom did, and go to college. He knew his mother was a graduate of M.I.T., but he wanted to go to the school with the most graduated astronauts—the United States Air Force Academy in Colorado. Although excited, his mother was apprehensive as she remembered her time at M.I.T. So, at sixteen, Daisy and Alexander packed up for the academy, stuffing the last of the boxes into his dad's car.

Daisy wanted to go on the trip to Colorado, but Thomas and Alexander felt it would give them the extra time they needed to bond.

Thomas had graduated from the academy and was so proud he couldn't wait to provide Alexander with the exclusive tour.

Alexander walked over to his mom and felt that driving away was impossible for a moment. But his mom smiled with her beautiful smile, and he knew everything would be okay. Final goodbyes said as Daisy stood in the middle of the street as the car drove off, watching her future and the world's future fade over the horizon.

Time pass by. Alexander graduated, and Thomas passed away while Alexander was a student. He was visiting family in New York when a tsunami hit the city. It killed half of the population of Manhattan. With Thomas gone, it was now just Alexander and his mother, Daisy.

One day, in the dimly lit kitchen of Daisy's home, Alexander attended to the oven, taking out food as the aroma filled the air. The tranquility was disrupted when Daisy stumbled into the house, visibly exhausted and on the verge of passing out. Alexander sprang into action, swiftly moving to her side and catching her before she could collapse.

Alexander guided Daisy to a chair, concern etched on his face. Despite her weariness, Daisy managed a soft smile as she gently touched his cheek.

This is what every day was like for years. They had to watch their backs every second, even though they were trying to protect the backs of humanity, an accurate picture of the challenges they faced in their relentless pursuit of humanity's salvation. The juxtaposition of the familial bond against the backdrop of global turmoil rewarded the sacrifices made in their commitment to the greater good.

Knight
Discoverer
from darkness
to light

12
The Lunar Station

The lunar station was facing its greatest challenge yet: ending the ship's construction that would follow the journey into a black hole. Daisy, fueled by a daring idea, sought a way to guide the ship into the black hole without succumbing to its immense gravitational pressure. Years of dedicated effort followed as Daisy relentlessly pursued this risky project.

The enormity of the task required massive quantities of resources. Thankfully, progress was made in harvesting oxygen isotopes and creating synthetic Munerium.

The success of the Knight Discoverer, humanity's collective hope, hinged on the strength of a single rocket. Daisy urged her team to ensure the vessel could resist spaghettification upon entering the black hole. Munerium's unique properties played a pivotal role in designing probes and rockets, offering the ship a fighting chance against the powerful gravitational pull of the black hole known for consuming or repelling everything in its powerful gravitational pull.

Yet, uncertainties persisted, with the fear that one minor element of failure could render years of work futile.

As the completion of the Knight Discoverer faced delays, frustration mounted on Earth. The deteriorating ozone layer and harsh environmental conditions fueled public resentment. Protesters outside NASA reflected the growing anger, demanding accountability for the perceived failure to deliver on promises of salvation for humanity.

In the harsh daylight outside NASA, the sun beat down on protesters gathered outside the facility. Daisy maneuvered her car through the gates, but the scorching conditions heightened tensions. As time passed by, Earth edged closer to becoming uninhabitable. The ozone was nearly gone, and being outside in the sun became self-torture. Nonetheless, some risked the oppressive heat to let their voices be heard.

Protesters, affected by the intense heat, demonstrated their frustration. A protester smashed the back window as Daisy's car moved through the crowd. Startled, Daisy accelerated away, leaving the agitated crowd behind, seeking refuge from the intense sunlight.

Meanwhile, the lunar space station, nestled within a crater on the Moon and overlooking Earth, stood as a colossal testament to human ingenuity. Dominating the landscape was a massive facility featuring a giant glass-enclosed orb that housed several small buildings. Adjacent to the orb, a colossal hangar nearly double in size loomed as a hub of activity.

A partially constructed Knight Discoverer occupied the center stage within the lunar space station's expansive hangar. Clad in the latest astronaut gear, a cadre of engineers and scientists meticulously toiled to assemble the spacecraft further.

The makeshift town housed scientists and engineers, featuring living quarters, a greenhouse, and a medical center. Here, beneath the protective orb, the lunar inhabitants lived and thrived. Periodic food shipments sustained them, supplemented by a greenhouse ensuring a steady supply in case of scarcity.

The lunar space station's mines were where workers clad in astronaut gear delved into the Moon's depths. With a gigantic drill beneath them, they collected Munerium, a crucial resource, to be transported to the hangar for the completion of the Knight Discoverer. The drill spun relentlessly, symbolizing the tireless efforts of those working to secure humanity's future beyond the confines of the dying solar system.

And so, the lunar space station stood as a beacon of hope, a testament to human determination, as it propelled toward realizing a new Earth—Canaan.

Moon Blessing

The completion was expected to take 25 years due to the complexity of the project and all the technological advances that needed to be implemented and invented to be placed inside such a revolutionary ship. Each stage and every inch of the ship needed careful design and strategic construction to withstand the impending pressures.

The spaceship finally landed on the Lunar Space Station. As the door opened, Alexander stepped out, gazing toward the orb, marking the beginning of a critical chapter in humanity's journey beyond Earth.

In the Lunar Space Station's training area, the young Alexander experienced the gravitational pull training simulator. Strapped in, his body shook against the wall as the simulator spun him rapidly. His determined expression transformed into a scream under the strain of the intense training.

Later, in the Lunar Space Station's cafeteria, Alexander collected food on a tray and settled at an empty table, visibly vexed. Sofie, a woman in her late twenties, observed his struggle and noted the judgmental gazes of other trainees.

Among the trainees, murmurs circulated about Alexander, asserting that his position was solely due to his mother's influence. Sofie, however, challenged their narrow judgments, suggesting a more empathetic understanding of Alexander's circumstances. She emphasized the importance of getting to know the person leading them to the new world.

Sofie, carrying her tray, approached Alexander's table, disrupting the tense atmosphere. She remarked on Alexander's mother's involvement in the space station's design, catching Alexander off guard. As he stared at her in a trance, Sofie asked permission to join him, and Alexander, still surprised, agreed. Introducing herself as Sofie, she extended a hand, and Alexander, somewhat flustered, shook it. The exchange was observed by other trainees who eyed Alexander judgmentally. Sofie then lightened the mood, acknowledging the prevalent belief among the crew that Alexander secured his position due to his family's successes. However, she assured him that she was joking and acknowledged the inherent challenges of leadership.

As Sofie continued the conversation, playfully touching Alexander's shoulder, they shared laughter, temporarily easing the tension. Alexander's defensive posture softened, and he invited Sofie to call him Alex. This began a connection that would deepen over the next three years.

In the subsequent period, Sofie and Alexander became inseparable. Their relationship evolved from friendship to a profound connection, becoming confidants and, eventually, lovers. Sofie's shy smile and a brush of her hair indicated the blossoming bond in the challenging environment of the Lunar Space Station.

Night fell in the quiet confines of Alexander's room on the Lunar Space Station as he immersed himself in a manual. The tranquility was disrupted when Sofie stealthily entered through the door. Alexander, reflecting on the station's strict policy against relationships until reaching Canaan, found himself unable to resist Sofie's allure. In a peaceful exchange, she straddled him on the bed, and the two shared a passionate kiss. Moments later, she observed pictures of his family on a shelf. Alexander acknowledged the significance of family, science, and faith in his life.

"How do you combine science and faith? Aren't they against one another?" Sofie inquired.

"On the contrary. They complement each other. They're part of the same world. What science can't explain...faith helps me understand," Alexander explained.

Reaching for the Bible on the shelf, he opened it to the Book of Genesis, narrating the chapter that outlined the universe's evolution. Puzzled, Sofie listened as Alexander connected scientific concepts with the ancient text.

"The science of evolution and the history in Genesis complement each other," Alexander elaborated. He marveled at how the Bible, written thousands of years ago, seemingly described the universe's evolution and life on Earth.

Sofie, intrigued, bit her lip, prompting Alexander to express his faith in God, inspiring the writing of the Bible—a testament to the creation of the universe and humanity's second chance on Canaan.

"I like it when you put it that way. It's romantic," Sofie remarked, prompting a smile from Alexander. Pointing to a framed poem, Sofie inquired about "The Pale Blue Dot." Alexander explained Carl Sagan's perspective on Earth's fragility and humanity's misbehavior.

"One can only hope we learn from our mistakes. All I know is that they have a great leader bringing them into this new world. Humanity is set up to thrive," Sofie remarked before the two shared a heartfelt kiss, sealing their connection in the vastness of space.

The Knight Discoverer had been built by the construction crew since 2110, and now, in the Lunar Space Station's hangar, Alexander stood before the completed Knight Discoverer, a nearly mile-long spaceship with a sleek, cigar-shaped design that gleamed from the Munerium used in its construction.

"The Knight Discoverer was finally complete. The design hopefully proves flawless," Alexander reflected, noting the ship's thin but robust structure essential for surviving the spaghettification process inside Sagittarius A. The passengers and crew would be positioned at the ship's thickest point, ensuring their safety.

Walking on the Moon's surface toward the orb,

Alexander paused, looking into the distance. Sofie stood at the edge of the crater, contemplating Earth's desolation. The once beautiful home now resembled Mars, a result of human greed.

"Our beautiful home was destroyed by human greed. Now... everything and everyone we've ever known will die with it," Sofie lamented, tears streaming down her face. Alexander, attempting to wipe away a tear, realized the obstacle posed by her astronaut helmet, leading to shared laughter.

"Canaan will be our new home," Alexander reassured Sofie. Concerned about the future generations of Canaan, Sofie wondered how to ensure they would avoid repeating Earth's mistakes.

"We'll make sure. I don't know how, but we will," Alexander affirmed, and Sofie took his hand. "Alex... I'm pregnant," she revealed. Shock turned into joy as Alexander's eyes widened, and a broad smile lit up his face. The couple embraced.

"Now all that was left was to go home, say our final goodbyes, and pick up the chosen humans for the journey," Alexander concluded in his thoughts, marking the beginning of the next chapter in humanity's quest for a new home.

13
Hard Decisions

Alexander, a member of the crew entrusted with managing the Knight Discoverer (KD), was chosen for this critical mission. The crew underwent extensive training on the Moon, eagerly anticipating the realization of their dream to utilize science for the salvation of humankind. In 2133, the crew, including Alexander, was poised to commence testing the equipment essential for their journey to the "Promised Land."

It was time to make the hard choices; all the accolades had been heard, but now it was time for reality.

Everybody wanted to survive the apocalypse and go to Canaan, a typical survival instinct as soon as society knew the spaceship would be launched in the next few years. However, the fear in people's eyes, trying desperately to find a way on the craft, grew more feral as every year passed. So driven to board the ship by any means necessary was the mission of billions of people.

Most people had nothing left except to create elaborate plans to sneak into NASA and enter the spaceship.

NASA had become a militarized zone bunkered

down. At the beginning of the twentieth year of the ship development, the entire mission control facility and all the team and crew members and their families were moved to a forty-story bunker underground to protect them. Once the selectees from the lottery are established, they, too, will be housed in the bunker. The most crucial strategy for protecting the spaceship was moving it and its construction crews to the Lunar Station. Then, not only will it be easier to have quality control over the ship, but there would also be a slim possibility of anybody hijacking the rocket.

Finally, Presidents and leaders of all countries randomly chose a committee of twenty people from across the world. The team represented all walks of life but not all countries. For the selection to work, the committee members were anonymous to each other (they sat with chaperones worldwide in secrecy), and none of the team members would be selected for the journey.

Hopefully, with the world's people on board with a system, those selected will face fewer challenges. However, the committee was optimistic at best; the world was in a frenzy.

The group themselves seldom went through a session without heated discussions – as they were deciding which 9.9 billion people would die on a dead Earth while 22,000 people flew off into space to a new, better planet.

A lottery system was eventually agreed upon by members without much fuss. It was the next step, and the criteria of who would be placed in the lottery chaos ensued.

Their selection process needed to be wholly defined and absolutely with no room for compromise; no matter one's wealth, influence, power, or connections, the lottery selectees will not change once they come from the computer.

Hot debates set the tone for the first meeting as each member tried to present their agenda. One consensus heard throughout the hall was determining the age of older people left behind. Some members wanted the cut-off point at seventy years old. Who would be there for them without relatives or anyone to protect them? On the other hand, some committee members argued people under seventy could be productive on the new planet since there are chores to be completed in people's homes.

As the arguments continued, the elderly number went down to sixty until the members eventually settled for the cut-off age of fifty. This final decision was the first to condemn millions to death at the hands of a toxic planet.

It was time for the conversation everyone had hoped to avoid, but each member agreed to be thoughtful and logical no matter the reality of their heartbreaking decision. It was time for the cutoff for the youngest. The panel discovered there were still too many young people to put in the lottery. The young adults in the lottery needed to be dynamic, childbearing, productive, and healthy. Again, the criteria used for deciding the future of the youth needed to be critical.

Argument after argument, the team finally decided twenty years or older would be placed in the lottery; the room was silent. How sad to end a day knowing only twenty thousand people had an opportunity to save humankind, and this committee decided the fate of the 9.9 billion people left behind.

The lottery placed names of all the inhabitants of Earth between the ages of 20 and 50 into a computer system where 10,000 males and 10,000 females were randomly selected to colonize the new world, Canaan.

In the bustling Mission Control at NASA, Alexander Silva assumed the role of Commander, overseeing the room as scientists diligently collected data.

As Alexander observed the room, an elderly Marlene approached with orders. They exchanged words, with Alexander expressing gratitude for Marlene's contributions.

"You deserve a room on this ship, and you'll have it. Without you and my mother, none of this would be possible."

Marlene, however, declined, acknowledging her capabilities but opting for another engineer. She cautioned Alexander about the challenges ahead and the press room awaiting his announcement.

"Thanks, Marlene," Alexander responded, taking a deep breath before proceeding to the press room.

In the NASA press room, cameras focused on Alexander standing at a podium, preparing to deliver crucial information. "Good evening...or I suppose I should say good morning, day, afternoon, and evening. Wherever you are in the world, thank you for tuning in," Alexander began.

He addressed the reality of the Knight Discoverer project, emphasizing the need for global preparation. Alexander revealed the Earth's dwindling population due to natural disasters and global warming, making the project necessary.

"The Knight Discoverer can safely house 22,000 people, so a selection process is needed. We unfortunately cannot take everyone. I'm sorry..."

He announced the government's decision that no person over fifty would be considered for selection based on the ability to work and contribute to the population of Canaan. The selection process would commence immediately, involving 10,000 men and 10,000 women chosen randomly.

"We thank you for your cooperation during this trying time," Alexander concluded, lowering his head as the weight of the announcement settled. The daunting reality of choosing who would be saved hung heavily in the room.

The ship's limitation was twenty-two thousand

people; two thousand were reserved for the International Space Command Center's crew members comprising scientists, engineers, technicians, military personnel, command crew, and families. The following 20,000 people would come from the lottery.

The spacecraft team would take care of all passengers, ensuring their safety. This mission, vital to the colonization of Canaan, was the last hope of humanity surviving extinction.

Everyone selected for the trip to Canaan was just waiting for Knight Discoverer to be completed and ready for launch in 2135.

<h1 style="text-align:center">14</h1>
<h1 style="text-align:center">Departure</h1>

Daisy was old at this stage. Even though her age was advanced now, the people around her and others not in her circles greatly respected her. They respected her because she was the ship designer. Her work of decades was finally going to help people escape problems compounding by each day on Earth —her ship would take them to Canaan, the promised land.

Because of her work, her son thought it was natural that she would be coming with them to the Moon for the final stages of the preparations, but he was to receive the shock of his life when he finally brought the subject up before her. Daisy was in her 50s when she gave birth to Alexander, and by then, she thought she was too old to participate in many things.

Amid a wild windstorm, a cloud of red dust engulfed the area of the neighborhood where Daisy lived. Alexander clad in an International Space Command Center (ISCC) uniform with a mask covering the lower part of his face, Alexander emerged into view and arrived with his transport. Surveying the desert climate, he furrowed his brow, witnessing the relentless force of nature.

Bending down, Alexander picked up a handful of sand on the ground and noted wearing a bracelet that bore the words "God's Blessings and Hard Work." Allowing the sand to trickle through his fingers, he turned his attention to an hourglass in his inseparable bag. Engraved on its base were the words "Time is Relative. Brilliance is Not. From Darkness to Light." He turned the hourglass, watching as the sand steadily descended into the empty chamber below.

Inside Daisy's home, in the living room, an elderly Daisy observed Alexander's actions from the window. As Alexander turned and headed back towards the house, Daisy sighed and sat on the couch.

Alexander opened the door, allowing the swirling sand to infiltrate the room. Quickly closing and locking the door behind him, he moved to the center of the room, unstrapping his mask.

"It's time to go. Are you ready?" Alexander stated with a sense of urgency. Meeting his gaze solemnly, Daisy slowly lifted her head, signaling the gravity of the impending departure.

Because of her work, her son thought it was natural that she would be coming with them to the Moon for the final stages of the preparations. "What tremendous honor it would be to be a part of your life's first and final mission?" Alexander thought. "Surely, she would love to be with her family as we look for a better tomorrow?"

Amidst all the chaos on the surface of Earth, he had little time to wonder about such things, to dream about the future life he would hold and cherish.

"Would things be different? Could things be better?

How will my grandchildren see our history?" So many thoughts with no accurate answers erupted into Alexander's mind.

Alexander Silva stared at the woman before him, his voice calling, "Mom?"

Daisy held a certain tranquility. "I'm not going anywhere, Alex. I turned down my seat a long time ago," she reassured.

Confusion and frustration played across Alexander's face. "But Mom... that's your ship! You designed and built it! I... I don't understand..."

"My work is done. I'm not going," Daisy responded with calm determination.

In disbelief, Alexander looked away and sank onto the couch, shaking his head in frustration. Daisy continued, "You know, I never told you this, but the same day that I found out I was pregnant with you, one of the drones from Carr sent us data. That was the data that informed us it had found a planet that was habitable by humans. It had found Canaan."

A beat of silence hung in the air before she added, "It gave me hope when all my hope was gone. It's why I named you Alexander."

Alexander, still perplexed, asked, "What does that have to do with anything?"

"Alexander means the savior of men. And here you are... the Commander of Knight Discoverer—humankind's last hope. The last hope of avoiding extinction," Daisy explained. "Do you think all of this is just a coincidence? It's not. This is God's plan. You were born for this mission and this purpose. I know you believe this."

Slowly nodding, Alexander finally admitted, "I do... but you should be beside me."

"My purpose is already complete, Alex. You're the next Silva up to complete our family's mission fully. Do you understand that?" Daisy questioned.

"Yes. I won't let you down," Alexander vowed.

"I know you won't. You never did," Daisy said, pausing. "We can talk about all the theories of the cosmos, all the mathematical equations to explain the universe and science, but do you know the thing that sums up the whole universe?"

Alexander replied with uncertainty, "No."

"Love, Alex. Love is the fundamental force that moves the universe and everything in it. It connects everything to it. It's more powerful than any force and faster than light. My love for you is infinite and eternal. It doesn't matter how far you are or where you are. My love for you will always connect us. God is love."

As Daisy spoke, Alexander fought back tears. She stood and moved towards him, and the two embraced.

As the sand from the top chamber neared its end, the hourglass trickled into the bottom.

In the moments that followed outside Daisy's home, she stood at the door, watching Alexander enter a car amidst a sandstorm. He glanced back at her before getting into the car, lowering his head in sadness. Daisy closed her eyes as tears ran down her face.

Alex stood confidently in front of his mother, but as the car started and he backed out of the driveway one last time, he wept. Not tears of solemn sorrow but of genuine pride. He must do the same if his mother could brave the threats put upon her.

Knight
Discoverer
from darkness
to light

15
Lift off

In the dimly lit Mission Control room at NASA, Alexander stood alone, his gaze tracing constellations of memories. Marlene approached. "I guess this is goodbye," she murmured.

Turning to face her, Alexander responded with a smile, and the two shared a lingering embrace. Marlene spoke again, her tone a mix of jest and sentiment.

"I'll be your cosmic companion, ensuring you have someone to talk to when you soar into the unknown. How about a little twist on the classic 'Houston... we have no problems' before lift off? That would be appreciated."

With a nod, Alexander assured her, "Will do, Marlene." After a contemplative pause, he added, "This isn't farewell; it's just a "see you later.'"

"Yeah. Until our paths cross among the stars," Marlene replied as Alexander turned away, heading toward the exit. She watched him depart, the room filled with a quiet anticipation of the odyssey ahead.

At NASA's launch site, Alexander observed from a distance as a crowd of 20,000 people was directed toward several shuttle rocket ships.

"Launch day has finally arrived. It's hard to be as excited as I was now, even though my mom won't be joining, but this is everything my family has ever

113

fought for. She was right. I was meant to be here."

Walking toward one of the rockets, Alexander spotted Sofie waiting at the entrance.

"Sofie," he greeted.

"Commander Silva. Welcome aboard the shuttle to the Knight Discoverer," Sofie replied. Alexander smiled and planted a kiss on her cheek. Together, they turned and walked onto the rocket.

Once everything was set in motion, distant spectators witnessed the shuttle spewing a blue flame, surrounded by an aura of raw energy. All the rockets ignited simultaneously, propelling upward toward the Moon. After a few seconds of the brilliant blaze, they vanished into the sky, leaving behind smiles and joy as humanity embarked on a new frontier.

In the interior of the rocket shuttle, Alexander and Sofie stood near a large window, silently observing the Moon growing more extensive in the distance. A shared smirk passed between them before they gracefully navigated through the crowd.

Moments later, all the rocket ships touched down almost simultaneously at the Lunar Space Station. The shuttles successfully transported the crew and other pioneers from Earth, landing on the Moon. A long glass-encased tube extended toward Alexander's ship, connecting to the exit.

As the door opened, Alexander took the lead, Sofie by his side, guiding the group off the ship and toward the Lunar Space Station. The journey to this uncharted frontier had truly begun.

Decisions

Standing at the dome entrance, Alexander took a deep breath of the oxygen produced and prepared himself for his role as captain. He marched onto the landing bay and began to speak to the passengers.

"Future settlers of Canaan," he bellowed, "Today, we mark the first step of our journey into the infinite! This Moon base is the last bit of home you will see for the rest of your natural lives; make sure to spend it wisely. We carry humanity's future to Canaan, and the light of our forefathers shines upon each one of us today."

Alexander takes a moment to contemplate, his mother's final words ringing through him like an empty stadium.

"You have three days to do everything you must before our journey continues; report back here once you're ready to depart." Alexander then waved at the passengers as many exited the station with PES systems, ready to explore the station.

"Does anyone have any questions to ask?" Alexander shouted at the top of his voice. All the remaining people stood silent.

"Captain?" a voice announced over his signal. "Behind you, sir," he spoke again.

Alexander turned, and before him was a woman he had never seen."The view is something, isn't it?"

"Nothing even close to the movies," Alexander

responded. The woman chuckled harder than he had ever seen someone laugh.

"You ever thought we'd see her like this? The whole thing is so huge and perfect?" the woman said. "Not exactly like this ... " Alex uncomfortably murmured. "I've been up here on the Moon a while, captain; I've seen this view dozens of times, and I think to myself what Canaan may look like. Will it be bluer than the sea? Brighter than the sun? What is it like to sit there like this? All things I can't wait to find out." The woman pauses for a second, then begins again.

"Every time I look at the earth, I see the sun, and every time I see the sun, I feel the Moon, and I think about a book, Living with the Stars; you ever heard of it?"Alexander shifts, knowing the text very well. He nods affirmingly.

"Do you think that's true?" she inquires. "Think what's true?"

"Do you think we're all made of stardust? I know it's a dumb question... but I always thought that was a cool idea. That humanity is just a bunch of destroyed stars with the right components to make us. To think we are all connected to the planets, the sun, Canaan." The woman breaks off from her rant and looks inquisitively at her captain.

Alex responds, "I find it sweet, the idea that all energy comes from one thing, and we're all here because of it. It makes me feel like I have a purpose and a duty bigger than mine. Most of my life, I've felt that way, but I never thought about that text in that way ..." He waits to collect his thoughts, but before speaking, the woman stands, "Well, sir, sorry to disturb you, best be getting back to the ship." The woman begins to move back to the ship but looks back at Alex and asks, "Do you think we'll make it to Canaan?" Alex stands as well, and with a nod of confidence, he replies, "We will."

The woman smiled and returned to the ship, Alex following close behind; eventually, they made it back to the vessel. Alexander was the Commander of the ship, and Sofie was his First Officer. The two were determined to make history together as they prepared to lead the people from the Moon station to Canaan. Everybody was ready to explore the new planet.

In the living quarters of the Lunar Space Station, Alexander stared out of his window, the Earth below appearing lifeless and distant. Holding a crucifix and a photo of him with Daisy from their younger days, he reflected on the past.

The door slid open, and Sofie entered.

"Hey," she greeted, the door closing behind her.

"Hey," Alexander replied without turning to face her. Sofie walked up, wrapping her arm around him and resting her head on his shoulder. She glanced at the photo.

"You know... you're fortunate. You could've lost both your parents," she remarked.

"In a way, I did," Alexander replied.

"You know what I mean," Sofie continued after a beat. "I know how you lost your Dad, but imagine losing both of your parents in a tragic way when you were much younger."

Alexander shifted his gaze to Sofie, and she recounted a painful memory.

"I watched it happen too. A fire ripped through our town, and we were surrounded. A helicopter somehow found us in all the smoke and blazes... and someone from the military climbed down a rope ladder to save us," Sofie explained. "My parents made me go first, and the soldier held me in his arms as he slowly ascended back up the ladder. Just as my parents were about to follow, the rope caught fire, too. They were trapped again."

She paused, lowering her head in sadness.

"I watched from above as the fire consumed them. I heard their screams... even over the roar of the helicopter's engine."

Moved by her story, Alexander turned and kissed her on the forehead.

"I'm so sorry," he said.

"Just know how lucky you were to have a mother who was

there until pretty much the end," Sofie said.

"I do. I'm even more fortunate to have you," Alexander replied. She slightly smiled and then took his hand, placing it on her stomach.

"Our child will be the first human born on Canaan," Sofie revealed. "Promise me you'll always be there with us."

"Sofie..." Alexander began.

"Promise me," she insisted.

After a moment's pause, Alexander responded, "I can't promise something I have no control over. The probe survived going into the black hole, but we're still taking a great risk."

"This isn't the time to be logical. I just need to hear the blissfully ignorant reassurance," Sofie pleaded.

Alexander chuckled and nodded. "Okay. I promise." They shared a smile and sealed the promise with a kiss. In the Lunar Space Station training area, Alexander stood at the front of a massive room, addressing the assembled crowd.

"The day of embarkment is upon us. After a few days of final preparations and teaching our chosen citizens imperative safety techniques, we were ready to leave our galaxy forever," he declared. His words echoed through the training area as the mission to venture beyond the galaxy reached a critical moment.

A brief pause filled the room.

Knight
Discoverer
from darkness
to light

16
Beyond

In the Lunar Space Station hangar, Alexander observed as the people and crew filed onto the Knight Discoverer.

Sofie approached, holding a tablet.

"Commander, were all final tests successful?" Alexander inquired.

"They sure were," Sofie replied, a confident smile gracing her face.

Alexander smirked. "Do you have your bag? I'll put it away in your quarters, and we'll meet at the control deck."

Alexander turned and picked up a small satchel. Opening it, he revealed an hourglass, photos of his family, and a Bible. "Be careful with the hourglass. It was my Great-grandfather's," he cautioned.

"I will. I'll see you up there," Sofie assured, taking the bag and walking away. Alexander watched her go, his gaze returning to the Knight Discoverer, the vessel that would carry them on their monumental journey.

In the control deck of the Knight Discoverer, Alexander sat in the Commander's chair while various Crew Members operated switches, pressed buttons, and monitored screens for readings. Sofie entered and took the empty seat next to him.

Rising from his chair, Alexander turned to address the Crew Members. A hush fell over the room as they directed their attention to him.

"Today marks the end of a long-awaited process of saving humanity. Our population dwindled throughout three generations, and everyone on this ship lost someone close to them. Some may have died long ago, some we may have left behind," he began.

A solemn pause hung in the air.

"We must be successful for not only them but for the future of our species. God has given us this opportunity, and we will not squander it," Alexander asserted.

Another beat passed as the Crew Members absorbed his words.

"We will take off effortlessly, effectively making our way through the wormhole, safely travel into and through Sagittarius A, and finally land in peace on our new home planet. Then, it marks our new beginning," he continued.

The Crew Members nodded with smiles, a collective sense of determination filling the room.

"Let's embark on this journey home!" Alexander declared. The Crew Members erupted into applause and cheers. Alexander returned to his seat and looked over to Sofie with a smile. She reached over, firmly grasping his hand, their connection symbolizing the unity and resolve of those on the Knight Discoverer.

The roof opened in the lunar space station's hangar, revealing the vast expanse of space. The engines of the Knight Discoverer roared to life, emitting a vibrant blue glow.

Alexander strapped himself inside the Knight Discoverer's control deck, and Sofie did the same. He gazed out of the window, taking a deep breath.

In the living quarters, the citizens strapped themselves in, their expressions reflect a mix of anticipation and worry.

Moments later, the Knight Discoverer levitated off the ground, slowly ascending into the air and out of the hangar. It hovered above the hangar for a few moments.

Alexander held the crucifix, his other hand on the launch button. He pressed it, and the ship immediately jolted and rumbled. In the vast space, the Knight Discoverer's exhausts shot out blue flames as it rapidly ascended, leaving the Moon's orbit behind. The journey beyond the stars had officially begun. The K.D. stretched upwards into the ever-consuming space, and soon, they found themselves going away from the Moon in the famous K.D. toward the great dark beyond.

For Alexander, the journey was necessary. Even though he had Sofie to talk to, she was his first immediate assistant. Their connection went beyond just themselves; it was a partnership dedicated to the well-being of everyone on board.

Simultaneously, at Daisy's home, she slowly made her way out of the house. The sandstorm had ceased, and the sky now revealed its clear expanse. As they transcended further into space, Daisy began to cough profusely.

"Miss, are you alright?" her caretaker exclaimed.

Daisy ceased her episode and responded with a voice akin to a sputtering car engine.

"I'm fine..." she paused for a moment, then asked a question. "Take me outside . . . I want to see my son make it to our new home." She collapsed as she tried to stand by herself. "Daisy!" her caretaker exclaimed. "Let me get you up,

Miss, let me help you."

"No!" Daisy shouted. "I will go outside, I will see that ship, I will wave goodbye to my son."

Both women ceased speaking as her caretaker knew Daisy was serious. "Okay, Miss, I will help you see him."

Daisy buckled under the world's weight but needed help to get up to the porch. She sits on her old rocking chair and feels the harsh breeze of warm dusty air perforate her face. Daisy gazed up at the Moon, and her eyes caught a sight—a blue orb streaking away from it, disappearing into the vastness of space. The departure of the Knight Discoverer didn't go unnoticed, even from the quiet surroundings of Daisy's home. In the control deck of the Knight Discoverer, Alexander gripped Sofie's hand tightly, gritting his teeth. He looked out the window, witnessing Earth shrinking in the distance. With a deliberate motion, he reached forward and pulled down on a lever.

The rumbling ceased, and the ship slowed to a casual cruising speed.

"Takeoff is complete. Ready the ship for the wormhole jump," Alexander announced. Crew Members quickly unstrapped themselves, moving efficiently around the area. Alexander sighed in relief and turned to Sofie.

"Onto step two," he remarked.

In the living quarters, citizens sighed in relief, engaging in conversations.

Moments later, a Crew Member approached Alexander and Sofie and reported, "Wormhole jump is ready, Commander."

"Good. Strap yourself back in," Alexander instructed. He reached for a microphone and addressed the citizens. "Citizens of Canaan, we're about to press onward and engage the wormhole. Please remain strapped in at all times." With the message conveyed,　Alexander　h e s i t a t e d momentarily before hovering his hand over the initiation button.

In Alexander's room, the hourglass sat on a table strapped down in the living quarters. The sand dripped down from the top chamber, nearly depleted, marking the passage of time as the Knight Discoverer prepared for the next phase of its journey.

Simultaneously, at Daisy's home, she looked up to the sky and saw the blue orb of the Knight Discoverer hovering amongst the stars. The distant sight of the spacecraft embarking on its interstellar voyage left an indelible mark against the cosmic canvas.

17
Final Journey

In the control deck of the Knight Discoverer, Alexander pressed the button. In the vastness of space, the ship emitted a powerful charge from the engine, shooting a beam of light forward. A wormhole twisted and opened up, revealing a brilliant swirling hole full of color. Alexander moved to the lever and pressed it forward. The ship entered the wormhole, swiftly swallowed by its cosmic embrace. As the Knight Discoverer disappeared into the anomaly, the wormhole rapidly closed, leaving behind the serenity of space. The journey through the unknown had begun.

Simultaneously, at Daisy's home, she watched as the orb in the blue sky suddenly disappeared. A deep exhale escaped her, and a solitary tear rolled down her cheek. The spacecraft's departure brought a mix of emotions, marking the beginning of an uncertain journey into the cosmos.

In the surreal expanse of the wormhole, the ship sped through the spinning colors, navigating the cosmic anomaly.

Inside the control deck of the Knight Discoverer, Alexander, and Sofie held their straps tightly as the ship rattled and shook. Within the wormhole, the focus shifted to one of the ship's engines—a continuous blue flame. Suddenly, it sputtered and came to a complete stop. Portions of the wormhole broke up, revealing flashes of the blackness of space.

Alex and Sofie continued their banter as usual. Suddenly, a robotic voice cried out from the intercom. "Engine room malfunction, ionic engine compromised, requires manual instantiation."

Panic arose within Alex's heart; he knew calamity was mere minutes away. An ionic engine overload was the last thing they needed for this mission; one faulty excess and the engine could jeopardize the ship's integrity down to the atom; the same problem the failed Allen probe, and Alex wouldn't let that happen again.

Back in the control deck, Alexander's eyes widened in horror as he watched the glitches in the wormhole through the window. An alert popped up on his screen, reading "Engine Failure."

"Oh my God," he muttered. Sofie nervously turned to him.

"What's happening?!" she exclaimed.

Unstrapping himself, Alexander declared, "Stay here!"

"Wait! Where are you going!?" Sofie protested.

Gripping onto his seat, Alexander pulled himself back towards the exit of the control deck. "Alex!" Sofie called out in desperation.

Moments later, in the engine access hall, Alexander

gripped the wall and pulled himself along until he reached the engine room door. Through the window, he saw two cords disconnected, sparks flying out of them. "Alex!" Sofie's voice echoed from behind him. He turned to see Sofie moving towards him. "I told you to..."

"What are you doing?" Sofie interrupted. Alexander sighed and looked to the engine room. "The same issue happened to the Allen probe my Mom launched. The engine became disconnected, and the wormhole was destroyed," he explained. "We only have one shot at this."

A look of realization crossed Sofie's face. "No..." she whispered.

"I have to go in there and manually connect it. They need to be put back into position at the same time. Otherwise, everyone will die," Alexander clarified.

Sofie sternly said, "I said no. You promised me."

Alexander looked back at her, caressing her face with one hand. "I said I couldn't make a promise," he replied.

"This is suicide! I won't let you!" Sofie protested.

"Sofie... it's okay. One should die for everyone to live," Alexander insisted.

"You don't have to sacrifice yourself !" Sofie pleaded.

"I'm the Commander. It's my duty... it's my purpose," Alexander explained.

Sofie's lips trembled, tears streaming down her

face. She shook her head and looked away. "I'm not ready to lose you," she confessed.

"And I'm not ready to lose myself as I lose you too in the process," Alexander responded, moving his hand down to her stomach and holding it there for a moment. He took off his necklace and placed it around Sofie's neck. "My love for you and our child is forever. No matter what happens, I'll always be with you both," Alexander declared. He lifted her chin, kissed her, and then stood before the engine room door. "Give me the wisdom and knowledge I need to make this decision. Make me follow your will. Amen," Alexander prayed. Reaching for the handle, Sofie pulled him back, and they embraced, sharing a deep kiss. "I love you forever," Sofie whispered. Alexander smiled, returned to the door, and opened it, ready to face the critical task ahead.

The unforeseen challenges of the journey had unfolded, and the crew faced a critical moment in the heart of the mysterious wormhole.

18

Reborn

Daisy was about to return home, but something held her. Quickly, she looked back up to the sky with a knowing worry. In the distance, the sun was about to rise.

"Alex..." she whispered, a sense of concern lingering in the air as the dawn approached, bringing with it the uncertainty of the unfolding cosmic journey.

Simultaneously, in the vastness of the wormhole, the ship glitched more severely as it wobbled.

In the engine room, Alexander closed the door behind him and latched it shut. Ahead, he saw a catwalk leading to a beam with disconnected wires flinging in the air. Undeterred, he moved forward.

Suddenly, a bright flash of light erupted, and Alexander instinctively ducked. Sofie peered through the window, banging on the door.

"Alex! Come back!" her muffled voice pleaded.

Alexander looked back at her, giving a thumbs up as reassurance. He then turned his attention forward and pressed on.

Reaching the beam, he looked down to see the inner workings of the engine—various gears and electricity moving and flowing. Taking a deep breath, he stepped out onto the beam, balancing himself and inching forward with determination.

Simultaneously, in Alexander's room within the living quarters of the Knight Discoverer, the hourglass contained just a minuscule amount of grains left. The sands of time were slipping away, marking the critical moments of the unfolding journey through the cosmic unknown.

In the engine room, Alexander reached the middle of the beam, looking up to see the two cords dangling and shooting out sparks. His fingers grazed the cord, just missing it. Waiting for the dancing cord to come back in his direction, he grabbed hold of it.

Turning his attention to the other cord, he reached forward to grab it but missed badly. Losing his balance, he slipped off the beam.

"Alex!" Sofie's muffled voice called out.

Gripping tightly onto the one cord, Alexander struggled to pull himself back up. Sofie banged on the locked door in desperation.

"Alex!" she pleaded.

Finally, Alexander pulled himself back up on the beam, holding the cord in his left hand. He looked to the other cord, timing it perfectly. Snatching it with his right hand, he held them both, glancing at the portion of the engine on either side where the cords came loose.

Alexander stretched his arms out, aligning the cords to be placed simultaneously. He screamed in agony, needing to stretch even more. Looking to his left hand where his bracelet dangled, a soft smile crossed Alexander's face.

"This is for you, Mom," he whispered.

Turning his gaze back to the window in the door, he saw Sofie sobbing. He smiled gently at her as she touched the window in sorrow. Then, he stretched his arms out and screamed, connecting the cords where they needed to be.

Simultaneously, in Alexander's room within the living quarters, the last drop of sand fell into the bottom chamber of the hourglass. The fleeting grains marked a moment of profound significance in the unfolding journey through the cosmic unknown.

In the engine room, a bright ray of blue light shot through the engine, engulfing Alexander. He was instantly vaporized by the intense energy, becoming one with the cosmic forces that powered the vessel on its interstellar journey.

Simultaneously, at Daisy's home, just as the sun rose and a gleam of light hit her eyes, Daisy gripped her heart.

"Alexander!" she exclaimed.

She collapsed on the ground and died instantly. The echoes of her cry resonated in the stillness of the morning, marking the end of Daisy's journey as the Knight Discoverer ventured further into the depths of the cosmos.

Two lives were claimed and soon returned to space, where they were once born and soon will be born again.

In the engine access hall of the Knight Discoverer, Sofie leaned against the door in despair.

"No! Alex...I," she began, her voice breaking. Sofie deeply sobbed, sinking to the ground in the grip of overwhelming grief.

Inside the engine room, Alexander's dust particles danced through the blue streaks of the engine, eventually being sucked out through the ventilation system. His essence, now dispersed, became intertwined with the cosmic energies that powered the vessel, forever a part of the journey through the vast unknown.

While watching this happening, Sofie stood there with her right hand over her belly. She did not know what to say. Her newly found lover just decided to sacrifice his life for those aboard the ship. The crew was stunned at the sight and sounds of the dead captain, but Sofie looked at his last gift. Sofie stood tall and spoke, "Look, lively colonists! Our future is almost here!" she stood firm as they looked upon her. Emboldened by Alex's words and steadfast in her resolve. She stood there, ready for the space jump. Alexander was a courageous man. He would have continued the mission when everybody else was safe.

Finally, the engine fell ok, and the wormhole encompassed the ship.

19
Three Saviors

In the control deck of the Knight Discoverer, Sofie, now seated in the Commander's chair, gazed at the immense black hole encircling it with golden light. Her eyes reflected exhaustion and a muted emotion.

"Ready when you are, Commander," a crew member announced. Sofie, her hand on the lever, briefly glanced at the crucifix in her other hand. "Give me the wisdom and knowledge I need to make this decision. Make me follow your will. Amen," she whispered.

As the ship traversed the black hole, turbulence shook it violently. Sofie, maintaining a steady gaze, pushed the lever. The fate of the Knight Discoverer and its remaining crew now hung in the balance, swallowed by the colossal black hole, Sagittarius A.

In the cosmic expanse near Sagittarius A, the Knight Discoverer faced the overwhelming gravitational pull of the black hole. The front of the ship stretched and thinned out, disappearing into the dark abyss.

The middle stayed intact, and the back end stretched until the entire vessel disappeared into the darkness.

Meanwhile, the living quarters were well

protected. The passengers screamed and wailed, sounds distorted and in disarray. The matter seemed to morph between forms on a microscopic level within mere seconds as chairs and various items were liquefied and erupted into solid expulsion. The matter seemed inconclusive, as though reality bent to the black hole, and all within its grasp were along for the experience. Soon, everything was finished as they sped through the Inner Event Horizon. Dazzling lights like the rays of many suns burst through the shuttle's windows, and colors beyond comprehension danced within the ship's inner hull as they blended into mixtures of spectacular images, like fireworks from Heaven.

Inside the control deck, Sofie witnessed the violent shaking of the ship. It felt as if trillions of stars were rapidly passing them by. Bright white and golden light streaked past them, creating a breathtaking spectacle. The light intensified, becoming blinding.

Sofie shielded her eyes as the ship was engulfed in the brilliance. All that could be heard was Sofie's breathing. Then, the blinding light subsided, revealing Sofie seated there. She lowered her hand and looked ahead in disbelief.

In the vastness of space, the ship soared through the new universe, heading towards two bright suns in the distance.

The light then erupted into a spew of bending matter that refracted upon itself and established a dazzling show of beauty that seemed to bleed from the walls themselves.

Then, upon the lights exiting their view, it was over. A new solar system awaited them in space. The cabin erupted in joy and wonder as they saw the planet soon to be their home, except for Sofie. She looked to the crucifix, fighting back tears. Finally, she felt strong and spoke, "We made it. We were officially in our new universe."

The Knight Discoverer had traversed the unknown, emerging on the other side of the black hole, marking the beginning of a new chapter in the cosmic journey to approach Canaan—an exoplanet resembling a slightly larger Earth with diverse land masses and oceans.

Sofie's voice echoed, " It won't take long, and we will arrive at our new home of Canaan." A momentary pause followed.

"It is hard to feel happy," Sofie thought, lowering her eyes. The weight of the losses, the sacrifices made, and the grief she carried made the prospect of this new life in Canaan a challenging journey.

In the cosmic void, dust particles floated in space, carried by the currents of the unknown. Alexander's body returned from whence it came. Dust is made up of burned-out embers of stars released into the galaxy in massive explosions billions of years ago. The same dust that's part of every human.

The celestial dance of stardust is a poetic reminder

of the interconnectedness of life and the cosmic cycle that bound every being in the universe.

The Knight Discoverer descended upon Canaan, gently landing in a clear grass area. Sofie, the first to step out, marveled at the breathtaking landscape.

A very emotional Sofie needed to speak to everyone: "We said that humanity needed a savior... but in reality, it had three. The first was Joseph. The second was Daisy. And our final savior was Alexander." Her words echoed the acknowledgment of those who played pivotal roles in the journey.

20
Canaan

The ship landed on the fresh soil of Canaan, its thrusters now silent, and its landing deck opened. While it was a dream come true for everyone, Sofie couldn't shake her bewilderment. Yet, she knew she had to remain courageous until the mission was completed.

Having successfully led the people through space and a black hole, Sofie understood that leadership was now crucial to complete the mission.

Stepping into Canaan, Sofie said, "All I did was finish what Alex started. They were the true saviors of humanity." She looked around in disbelief, taking in the magnificence of Canaan—a picturesque Garden of Eden with lush grass, crystal blue skies, and clear water.

Canaan was covered with oceans, lakes, and exuberant forests. A beautiful planet composed of huge hills and deep valleys, mountain peaks, and deep flowing rivers, everything they could have ever dreamed of. The atmosphere there was breathable for humans, and they felt the difference, a far cry for people running away from polluted air. The planet was exuberant with natural beauties, reminding them of the Earth when it was still in its best days – before human activity ransacked the world's many wonders. As they looked at this newfound land, they could only hope they would take better care of this new Eden.

After discovering the challenge waiting for them, the people pitched tents nearby as they went to sleep. The night came swiftly after their landing, and the Moon filled the night sky with a dazzling spectacle of stars and celestial bodies. A sight so pure and breathtaking that many new inhabitants found rest wouldn't come quickly. Many could be heard twisting and turning throughout the night after the long voyage.

Those who chose to celebrate with more sensual activities saw this as an opportunity to delight themselves with acts of passion for their loved ones. Who would blame them? They were in a new area; no one knew what would happen to them the following day. The new colony of humanity ensured its first breathtaking night was one they would not forget.

The next day came, giving Sofie's crew a chance to begin a new day in this place. They were delighted to see that the sun rose just as it did on Earth, almost as if the planets were mirror images of each other, too perfect to be accurate, and yet it was. The day cycle went as expected; hours passed, and the colonists began to explore and settle in; many found various creatures unseen by human eyes before towering beasts and tiny critters darted the planet's trees and valleys.

Flora and fauna thrived here, everywhere to be seen. It was akin to that paradise. Everyone went to feel like they were in heaven, all except Sofie. The sun began its descent onto the horizon, marking the end of the first actual day for the settlers and Sofie. This was the first sunset in Canaan, and she wished to experience it alone, in total awe of the majestic journey she had almost completed it.

While looking at the beautiful two-star sunset from JSA and AFDATA, both fading behind the evergreen landscape, she grabbed Alexander's necklace and put her hands over her womb. She felt hope again. She thought about her child's future, watching the stars etch their final ray of energy across the skies of Canaan. Sofie reached her feet and walked away from the cliff into her new family's warming campfire and joyous laughter. She smiles and walks into the blazing light with pride and poise, ready for what tomorrow may bring.

As time passed, the grassy area transformed into an encampment where most Citizens now lived. Many settlers broke off into irrigation parties, and others established a setup for their first structures. Many more spread out into the far reaches of the plain they landed upon, hoping to discover new things with each step. Most people stayed within their landing zone, but a few brave souls strayed away to explore their new land.

The promise of exploration and the forging of a new life in Canaan began for the survivors of the cosmic odyssey.

In her quarters, Sofie, now with a full pregnant stomach, wrote in her journal, "Though we are still human and bound to make mistakes, I have hope that this time, mankind will learn its lessons and be gentler and wiser with this new home, this new beginning."

Sofie looked at the hourglass, a symbol of time and cyclical existence, turning it upside down. The sands began their journey anew—a reminder of time's passage and the continuous circle of life in Canaan.

On the grounds of the Canaan encampment, Sofie walked to a ledge overlooking a lush valley. Two suns set in the distance, painting the sky with a brilliant sunset. Holding Alexander's necklace, she placed it on her pregnant stomach, a serene smile gracing her face.

Back in the command room, Sofie sent her final message to Earth: "This is Sofie Silva, surrogate Commander of the International Space Command Center's Knight Discoverer, signing off." With these words, she marked the end of one journey and the beginning of another—a journey of hope, renewal, and the promise of a better future on the tranquil exoplanet Canaan.

To be continued

Knight
Discoverer
from darkness
to light